CRAVING HIS SPOTLIGHT

KAPOW SERIES, BOOK #3

RENÉE DAHLIA

Copyright © 2020 by Renée Dahlia

Print ISBN: 978-0-6489626-2-5

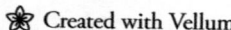 Created with Vellum

CRAVING HIS SPOTLIGHT

RENÉE DAHLIA

Can a second chance at fame avoid repeating old mistakes?

Pop star RILEY MICAH is at a cross-roads in his life. As a teen he found fame as lead singer for So You Think, but he lost it all in a haze of alcoholism. He's been clean for eight years, absolutely bloody sober. Working in outback Australia made him lean and tough but unsatisfied musically. A tune he uploaded online under a new name gets airplay on the radio, and he has a decision to make. Can he go back to life as a famous musician? If he tells people that Riley Le Breton is Riley Micah, the old lead singer for So You Think, the song—and perhaps his music career—will take off. But at what cost to his sober self? He needs a marketing plan to help him control it all; the money, the message, the impact on his sobriety.

Arrogant CEO VINCE CATTANEO has spent over a decade getting rich. No one would ever suspect the owner of Kapow Marketing spent the last years of his teens driving a beat up old car with a radio that wouldn't work and a CD stuck in the player. So You Think; on repeat for two years. If he never hears those songs again, it'll be too soon. When one of the band members walks into Kapow needing a marketing plan to deal with sudden new success, Vince is surprised at the way his voice resonates with him. The sudden spotlight on both of them will force Vince to confront the secret that drives him.

ABOUT THE AUTHOR

Renée Dahlia is an unabashed romance reader who loves feisty women and strong, clever men. Her books reflect this, with a side note of awkward humour. Renée has a science degree in physics. When not distracted by the characters fighting for attention in her brain, she works in the horse-racing industry doing data analysis and writing magazine articles. When she isn't reading or writing, Renée spends her time with her partner and four children, volunteers on the local cricket club committee, and is the Secretary of Romance Writers Australia.

CONTENT WARNINGS

Alcoholism, addiction.

ACKNOWLEDGMENTS

I pay my respects to the Wangal people of the Eora Nation, who are the traditional owners of the land on which this book was written. I also pay my respects to the Ngemba people of the Gurnu – Baakandji Nation, who are part of the Wongaibon Aboriginal language group. They are the traditional owners of the land around Bourke.

Thank you to my sister Tash and bro-in-law Scott for their hilarious small town step-grandmother "problem" that caused a short moment of panic until the genetic components of the relationships were figured out and they weren't actually related to each other by blood. Being your own step-cousin is more likely than you'd think, especially in a small town.

Thank you to all my readers. I'm honoured that you've spent your precious time on one of my books. Thank you to my fellow authors who've kept encouraging me on this writing journey, especially Lina Rivera and MV Ellis.

For second chances.

1

Vince would know that voice anywhere. The rich dulcet smoky voice with sultry notes. Truly, it was the only good thing about the bloody pop beat of those songs. For two long years, he'd listened to it on endless repeat, because there was no other option. Hearing that voice meant only one thing—the lead singer of So You Think was here in the office of Vince's advertising company, Kapow. It must be over a decade since the boy band was huge. He shuddered. That fucking car with the So You Think CD stuck in the dash represented some of the worst years of his life. Nah, not the absolute worst. They were the end of the worst and the beginning of now.

Reframe your thinking, that's what he always told his clients. Pivot. Imagine the outcome. One cheap unbreakable Toyota, and that bloody band, marked the moment he'd given himself the choice to be something more. To be the CEO of his own company and rise from the trash of his childhood. He'd achieved it all. The kicker was that he still wanted more.

Anna tapped on the glass door to his office, interrupting him before he could get carried away. What was it about that voice?

"Yeah?"

His PA had a giddy look on her face with a huge grin and glowing eyes. "Riley Micah is here."

He nodded and almost said, *'I know. I heard his voice.'* "Send him in." He would not roll his eyes at her joy just because he found the whole thing awkward for reasons he didn't want to discuss with anyone.

"You know who he is?"

"I am aware of pop culture, Anna." It was literally his job to be aware of all the trends.

"OMG. Do you know what this means?" She actually bounced, and Vince had never felt older than right at this second, much older than his twenty-eight years.

"That the conspiracy theories are wrong and he's not dead?"

"Can I put that on the Kapow socials?"

"No." Vince wanted to sigh, and he never bloody sighed. Instead he unclenched his jaw. Odd, he didn't remember clenching it. "Not until we know why he's here and what he wants. There's no good sense in pissing off a potential client before we've signed them up."

"Right. Well, you're the boss. You'd know best. I'll just get him, shall I?"

"Yes please Anna. And perhaps stick around in case we need notes taken." They wouldn't need notes. Vince had a spectacular memory. He did have one weakness; or more accurately, it was the weakness he'd readily admit to. He liked making people smile, and Anna's smile warmed him. She ran out of the room and he went to stare out of the large glass window at the city. Nothing made him feel lonelier than Christmas in Sydney—all those people with families doing stuff normal things together. How fucking maudlin. That bloody voice singing out happy pop tunes with an upbeat baseline had pulled him back to a part of his life he'd rather keep buried, a past he'd worked his arse off to escape. Anna's tap on the door dragged him back to the real world and he plastered on a smile as he turned around.

Well, fuck me dead. No wonder fans had screamed for Riley. The man was spectacularly handsome. A rush of dry heat swept up his spine and it took all his effort not to lick his suddenly dry lips. Short black hair, long limbs, lean muscles under a casual shirt with jeans that clung to strong thighs. His face had weathered since his boy band days, but it added substance to his classically beautiful features. Vince could understand why they'd made him the front man for a boy band. He had it all; incredible good looks, a lush voice, and a presence about him that made Vince want to follow him. He never wanted to follow anyone.

"Ahh, Vince, this is Riley Micah. He wants to see you on some business." Anna's quiet tone whipped at him, and he blinked. Had he been staring hungrily at his potential new client? Shit and balls. He squared his shoulders, marched across the room, with his hand stuck out for a handshake. He gripped Riley's hand and shook it. Another shot of heat raced up his arm, and he tensed rather than scuttle away like a scalded cat.

"Riley Micah. I'm Vince Catteneo. Welcome to Kapow. What can we do for you?"

"It's complicated." Riley's voice purred over Vince's skin and his toes nearly tapped out the beat to Vegas Showgirl where Riley sang those same words. *She's complicated. I'm complicated. The whole situation… well, it's complicated.*

"Isn't most of life? Ha ha." Oh fuck, now he was the dickhead saying that out loud. "Would you like a coffee? Anna can get you anything you want."

"No thanks. Water is fine."

With any other uptight potential client, Vince would have turned on the charm and wooed them. But someone had turned the aircon up too high and the room was too stuffy, and he couldn't find the words he needed. Routine. That's how to cope with the unknown. Take a breath, go through the standard welcome chat.

"Please have a seat and we can discuss your complicated problem. Our discussion is completely confidential, and we guarantee that regardless of whether you sign on with Kapow or not. Kapow is in the business of solving complicated problems for clients and we have an excellent track record." This was where Vince would casually indicate the wall of awards on display in his office, but something held him back. He eased out a slow breath as Anna placed clean glasses on coasters on the table in front of them both, poured iced water into them, and then sat down.

"How much do you know about the music industry?"

"About as much as I need to know to help you." Vince

paused, waiting to gauge Riley's response but he sat poker faced. "I realise that sounds flippant and it's not meant to be. We are in the business of advertising. We understand people and their motivations. We are experts in knowing why people spend money. If we need to understand a particular industry for a client, then we have a research team for that. What I'm saying is that if you need me to know everything about the music industry, come back in a week, and I will know it."

"Okay?" Riley was apparently a man of few words.

"I take it this has something to do with So You Think?"

Riley frowned, with a deep furrow between his brows. "You know about that?"

"Anyone alive a decade ago would have to be living under a rock not to know." Vince had been sixteen when the first So You Think song had been released. It hadn't really been his scene. He'd been into angry music, not happy pop, and it wasn't until he bought that damned car that he'd truly listened to their music. Totally not his thing. He wouldn't have listened to that CD, except he'd had no other option. At the time, it had been an analogy for his life; one that he'd used as motivation to give himself options and create opportunity.

Riley lifted his chin and spread his arms wide. "Perhaps my problem is not so complex, after all. I've been writing some new songs and one of them has some airplay." He paused, opened his mouth, then closed it again. Vince ran a few scenarios through his head. Which was more likely?

"I take it you've used a different name?"

"Yes. Riley Le Breton."

Anna gasped. "OMG, I've heard that one on Triple J. That's you? Man, when the world knows that, you are going to be huge."

Riley cleared his throat. "You guarantee me confidentiality?"

"Absolutely. And that includes all my staff. This will NOT leave this room. Anna?"

Anna squeaked. "Yes boss."

"Here's the deal. The music industry thrives on hope. When So You Think was formed, well, manufactured, whatever... The three of us were so happy to be famous, we signed the contract without really knowing what it would mean. A million dollars up front sounded like a fucking fortune. Sorry."

"It's fine. This is advertising. We do use swear words on occasion." Vince cringed a little inside; he sounded like a complete tosser. Anna giggled.

"Right. Well, we got fucked over, basically. No one told us the advance wasn't real money. All our expenses came out of it; like they paid us a daily allowance, and paid for all our travel, and clothes, and fucking everything. And all of it came from the original million they'd given us. So much for generosity."

"What about royalties?"

"By the time the producers and song writers and the music company had taken their cuts, we got almost nothing in percentage terms. Less than 4% of net profits, and when the music company did the accounting..."

"There wasn't much in the net profit line?" Vince guessed and Riley nodded.

"After three years of constant touring, So You Think was the biggest boy band in the world, we'd sold out concerts everywhere, we had platinum records, industry awards, all of that shit. And for all of those millions of records we'd sold, we were almost broke. And it broke us. Well, you've read the stories, I'm sure. How we went from the glamour boys to dust in three years."

Vince had no words. He thought advertising was a cut-throat industry, but fuck. "That's fucked up."

"Yes. I can't do that again." There was a weight to Riley's voice that asked more questions than it answered. Somehow Vince knew he didn't just mean the whole being famous without being rich, but that something more had happened in the intervening years. His team would fill in the details for him.

"And you want us to prevent that?" Vince wasn't sure how they could help.

"No. This time around, I will be the producer, the song-writer, the singer. I will create the wealth, if I'm so lucky as to hit the charts again, and I will keep it."

"Great." He waited, still unsure about why Riley had come to an advertising agency with his issue.

"What I need is someone to manage the public and the publicity for me."

Vince was tempted to brush Riley away and send him to a PR company instead, but he'd always been good at sniffing out business, and from the look of awe on Anna's face, he knew it wasn't just him who found Riley appealing. Sexy. If he could put his own physical response aside, Riley could be a valuable client.

"You want us to manage your fame for you?" His guess was spot on. Riley's face lit up, his brown eyes glowing and a smile slowly unfolded over his features.

"I've been there. I know how wild it can get, and as soon as anyone finds out that Riley Le Breton is really Riley Micah from So You Think, things are going to get out of hand. I want Kapow to launch Riley Le Breton in a way that manages the So You Think fans, but keeps the focus on the music and who I am now."

"And who are you now?"

Riley chuckled. "If I knew that, I wouldn't be here."

"I don't think that is true, at all. I think you know precisely who you are and what you want." Vince leaned forward, his elbows on the table.

2

Riley wasn't going to tell this man exactly who he thought he was. A washed up thirty year old ex-pop singer, a sober alcoholic whose fans thought was dead. There was a whole industry dedicated to that; websites, blogs, social media accounts, faux-headstones. The advice that you should never google yourself held true. He'd been okay not knowing, but as soon as his Riley Le Breton song had gained air-time on Triple J, he'd decided to have a look on the internet. Only to discover he was dead. In hindsight, he should've listened to the generic advice. It was quite unsettling.

In a different way to being here, in an advertising agency with Mr Catteneo. They made men differently in the city. Mr Catteneo stared at him with his dark brown eyes focused only on Riley as if he were the most important person—the only person—in the world. On anyone else, it would be flirting, if you could call this intensity flirting. Riley had obviously spent too long in the outback if this slick suited handsome advertising executive made him hot under the collar. The way he leaned forward on the table inspired dirty thoughts, especially with his shirt sleeves rolled up to his elbows, and his muscular forearms exposed. Riley could lick him. Prickles of heat burst on his cheeks and he swallowed.

Who was he now? That'd been the question, hadn't it? "I'm a singer. I want to make music that makes people happy. That's all I've ever wanted." It was some of the truth, enough of the truth for this conversation. Riley certainly wasn't going to tell this intense man the truth; he'd been so fucked up on alcohol and drugs that he'd lost touch with everyone who mattered. He'd ended up in Bourke in outback NSW, broke and broken.

"And astute enough to know that making people happy results in income for you."

Riley swallowed down the bitter taste at the back of his mouth. It wasn't his first time around this particular circus. "If I play this right, my music can make people happy…" It was the most understated way he could manage to explain the rapturous joy he gained from singing for people. No drug ever gave him the same high. "…and I get to control the money."

"Understood." The look on Mr Catteneo's face proved he did in fact understand. "We can run through the details of how the money works later and see if our lawyer Ella can make the deal better for you."

"It's fine. Now that music is all digital, the big companies have less power. I can be my own record label."

"But that means doing all your own marketing, shelf placement…"

"Shelf placement? No one buys physical music anymore. I can manage the uploads myself." He didn't need tech help. What he needed was distance from the So You Think fans, and someone to stop him falling off the wagon. No, he could do that if he had control over, well, everything. No surprises and definitely no parties. That would be the key.

"Okay. Like I said earlier, I'll have a better understanding of the music industry next week. Anna, write a note to get the market research done on indie labels."

Riley's chest warmed and then a cold shiver raced across his scalp. He knew this sensation—the moment when he was being charmed by someone who wanted something from him. "No thanks, Mr Catteneo."

"Please call me Vince. No to the research, or to us helping you manage the media announcement? As you said yourself, once the public finds out, it's going to get a little wild. We can look after all that for you so you can concentrate on your music." Vince's eyes narrowed a little and then he held up his palm. "I can see you have some doubts—"

Riley nodded. He sure did and it was difficult to remember why he'd come here in the first place. Vince was only saying what Riley knew was true. He did need someone to deal with the fans so he could write, sing, and perform.

"Everything will be done at your request. You will have complete control over the messaging and how your image is portrayed. What I meant is that we will provide a service to you to assist you in how you want to tell the world about yourself."

"I don't need to be sheltered." Although he did, and fuck, part of him wanted this gorgeous man to be all heroic and protective. He'd hardly been a saint in the last decade, although the opportunities for one-night stands without the entire town knowing had been scarce in Bourke. Small towns had many advantages, but the disadvantage was that everyone was in everyone's business. He'd pretended he was Paul Micah, Riley's cousin, for so long, he'd almost forgotten what it was like to be Riley Micah. Plain old boring old Paul, as the song went. The town bought it—'Oh you look just like him'—and then left him alone. He'd nearly believed the lie, except he'd stepped back into his old self with ease today. His stomach cramped. He couldn't go back to being Riley Micah, but he also knew his mates in Bourke would be gutted when they discovered he'd been lying to them. They'd cover the hurt with silly jokes, sure, but he couldn't pretend everyone would know he didn't trust them with the truth.

Vince chuckled. "No, I don't imagine you do. You have the look of someone worldly who knows exactly what vultures are out there."

Riley's pulse skipped a beat. "I'll take that as a compliment." Being here made his decision to reveal himself so incredibly real, even though he'd spent months thinking through all the implications. Theory had nothing on this twisting tornado in his stomach.

"You do that." Vince's gaze didn't budge, somehow inviting Riley to sink into those brown eyes of his. Riley could write a song for this man and it would be soulful with long notes and a deep bassline. A little bit of jazz with a sharp electronica intro.

"Thank you."

"I've talked a fair bit about what Kapow can do for you,

so tell me, Riley. Do you think this is a relationship that could work for you?"

Yes. Imagine being in bed with this man and the glory of being watched by those incredible eyes. Riley blinked. He hadn't meant that sort of relationship. "Should we talk about the cost?"

"We can get to that. I'm sure you've done your research about us and our services."

Riley nodded once. "Your website doesn't have any pricing information. I shortlisted you for a couple of reasons." He deliberately glanced at the impressive display of awards along one wall. Should he mention that they had underground parking, so he could drive here without being seen by the public? No.

"Pricing depends on what package you want. Do you want the basic advertising package? A website, basic promotion of your new album, etc. Or do you want more of a PR deal where we also manage your media time? I'm picking the combination will be the most useful to you, given the media frenzy that will happen once the link between So You Think and Riley Le Breton is discovered."

"I don't want it discovered. I want to announce it."

"Control the story. Perfect."

Yes, and more than that. Riley wanted to control the hysteria before it controlled him. He'd already drafted a text to all his mates back at work in Bourke. It would have to be enough for the moment, an inadequate way of thanking them for keeping him level over the past eight years.

"Excuse me." The PA interrupted in her breathy voice, like she might burst with the excitement of being in the same room as him. God, he'd become a cynical old fuck. Coldness surrounded his chest and he tried not to roll his eyes.

"Yes?"

"Have you talked to the other members in So You Think about this?" Her sharp question made his stomach sink. This was going to affect so many people.

"Not yet."

"We will need to prepare them for this news, with a confidentiality clause, otherwise this will get out of hand quickly. Do you keep in touch with them?"

Riley breathed out slowly to try and calm his galloping pulse. There was no easy way to say this, so he just spat it out. "They both work for the company who originally signed us. Ethan is a songwriter, and Dylan finished his MBA and is an executive there."

"Can you trust them?" Vince aimed for his jugular. Direct. Fucking sexy. A shiver rushed up his spine.

Riley wanted to say yes. "I'm not sure. We went through a pretty tough time together and that experience sticks with you, but..." He'd been a complete jerk to them both and it'd been years before he was well enough to reach out to them again. Now they had a very cautious relationship where they texted each other every few months, but nothing deeper. Hardly a friendship, although they'd probably understand the situation he was in.

"Understood. They work for a company who'd be pretty keen to re-sign you. Would you?"

Riley was glad he'd spent months trying to figure out the

answer to this one. "Look. I'm not going to rush into anything, but if they offered me the right sort of deal, then I'd be silly not to consider it. I'm just not looking for the sycophantic bullshit that goes with all of that. Indie suits me at this stage. It means I have to pay for all the costs upfront, marketing, artwork, video production, etc, but I don't have to do anything I don't want and I don't have to listen to their ideas about how it should happen."

"That's clever. And it perfectly encapsulates why you need Kapow; to do the market placement, media management, and advertising that a big label would usually do."

"Yes." A big breath rushed out past Riley's lips, drying them out. "That's precisely it." He should've opened with that, rather than let them dictate the conversation. He was so out of practice at being in this world—things were simpler back in Bourke.

"One last question."

"Yes?"

"How much time do you have before someone puts the two names together?"

Riley squirmed. "What do you mean? No one will connect the two."

Vince shifted a little, and his mouth twitched at the corner. "Riley Micah, Riley Le Breton. And it's hard to disguise your voice. You sound the same as you did back then."

A buzz started in Riley's ears. Vince had recognised his voice? He'd assumed no one would do that. Crap. "But most of my fans think I'm dead."

"I'm going to assume we don't have much time. Today is

Monday. Let's book a radio interview for Thursday morning."

Riley's breath caught in his throat. "So soon?"

"Thursday is the best day for press releases. It'll get the most attention, and it's Wednesday evening in America, which is also good. That gives us today to go through the contract between you and Kapow and three days to create a logo and website for you."

Riley knew this feeling. It was like being struck across the knees with plank of wood, sudden and jarring. Was he ready? Would he ever be ready?

"And I'm pretty sure if we waited another week, Anna might burst." Vince grinned at his PA and she giggled.

"It's true. I want to ring my mam and tell her. I won't. I won't. Promise. But wow. This is so exciting." Her thrilled reaction reminded Riley why he was doing this. He wanted to make music and make his fans happy. Seeing videos of So You Think fans in tears about his death had slayed him. It still made his eyes prickle with uncomfortable heat. Would they forgive him, even though he hadn't started the rumour? He'd done nothing to stop it either.

"Thursday it is."

Vince's smile was worth it. He glowed. There was no other way to explain it. "You won't regret it. Now Anna, can you please get Ella? We'll go over our basic contract, then make the adjustments you wish."

"That sounds good." Riley pushed away the flutter in his gut. He'd given this plenty of thought and he wanted it. The alternative was to fade into an ordinary life. It had its appeal, but it wasn't enough for him. Music spoke to him, it begged to be released into the world, as much a part of him as the beating of his heart. And to achieve that he needed support; support he was willing to pay for. It didn't help that Vince was so incredibly gorgeous, in an intimidating way. He wasn't classically handsome, not with that cragged nose, and angular features. It was more the way he commanded the room and spoke with complete confidence in his ability to solve all the Riley's problems. And boy, did he find that seductive. Almost too seductive for a working partnership.

3

Thursday morning came along far too fast. Riley had spent the last three days locked in various offices at Kapow going through so many details. Every single piece of information they needed for this announcement had been collated, investigated, brainstormed, until the perfect website had been created and the precise words written for this morning. They'd made sure his Riley Le Breton song was uploaded on all platforms for fans to buy, and the website would go live at the beginning of his interview. The preparation had far exceeded his expectations; to be fair, so had the price, but he could see the benefit he'd gain. He'd maxed out his credit card to pay the initial amount to Kapow and now he hoped it would all be worth it.

As he stood in the studio waiting room, he shook out his hands and ran through a few breathing exercises. It'd been years, literally, since he'd performed, and yet his body remembered the buzz of initial nerves and the ways he'd dealt with them. What he wouldn't do for a drink to take the edge of though. No. Fuck. He'd rather stumble in an interview than end up there again. His pulse raced.

"You okay? Remember I'll be with you the whole time." The rich tone of Vince's voice whispered over his skin, and Riley nodded.

"It's fine. Fine." It wasn't fine. One pesky thought about a drink to ease his nerves was the beginning of a relapse. Eight years sober. His breath tripped and fluttered over his lips as he tried to slow his galloping pulse. When he'd uploaded the Riley Le Breton track it had been a deliberate choice. He couldn't keep living without music, and he'd learned tactics to maintain sobriety. Now he needed to implement them because even though he was returning to the music industry, he couldn't let himself to return to old habits. He wouldn't survive.

A staffer popped his head in the room. "We are ready for you now." He waved and they both followed him down the hallway until he opened a door. "In you go. They aren't on air, so they'll ask you a couple of questions, then we'll get into it."

Vince walked in first, and Riley tugged his hat tighter around his ears, thankful that Vince had scripted this part too.

"Riley Le Breton?" One of the women in the studio asked.

"I'm Vince Catteneo, Riley's PR person. This is Riley." Vince waved in his direction and as they'd rehearsed, Riley kept his head low. His heart was beating so loud he was sure everyone could hear it.

"Okay?"

Riley could feel Vince's smile even without glancing his way from the way the two women hosting the show's eyes widened.

"We have an announcement to make, when you are ready."

"Oh?"

"You'll love it. I promise." Vince and his bloody confidence sent a rush of heat to Riley's cheeks and he was so glad they'd decided he should hide himself as much as he could until the perfect moment. The on air light lit up. "That was Weekend Hustler by Unearthed singer Riley Le Breton and he joins us now in the studio."

"Welcome Riley. Our listeners have been loving this song of yours. Do you have any others planned?"

This was his moment and he couldn't move. Oh shit. Silence. On radio which was the ultimate PR crime and one he'd had drilled into him so many years ago. He cleared his throat. "Thank you so much for having me. You'd think I'd be better at this whole interview thing." The script. This wasn't what they'd practiced. One of the hosts gave Vince a dirty look as if to say, we were told this was his exclusive first interview.

"I'm sorry. I'm a little nervous. This is my first interview as Riley Le Breton, but—" He pushed his hat back, and lifted his face to stare at the hosts. "—You might remember me."

They gasped and he smiled. Not the cocky smile they'd practiced, but he hoped it was close enough.

"It's been a long time since I was in a studio; eleven years to be precise."

"Riley Micah from So You Think?" Oh, thank fuck. They did recognise him just as Vince had said they would. It'd been a huge risk not to prep them, too much of a risk, but now they had recognised him, the flutter in his stomach disappeared and his smile grew.

"Yes. I'm pleased to announce that I'm not dead, just matured a bit. Like a good wine, I guess. I've been on hiatus and I'm so thrilled to hear that your listeners have been loving my Riley Le Breton tune." That bit had been from the script.

"It's funny you know. Every time we play Riley Le Breton, we get messages on our text line from people convinced that it's Riley Micah. I read one of them out once, and we were spammed with links to that commemoration website of yours all day."

Riley shrugged one shoulder. "Not my website. I had no idea those websites even existed until a couple of weeks ago. It's pretty amazing how many blogs are dedicated to my disappearance from the music scene." He shook his head. "I really shouldn't have looked myself up on the internet. It was something of a shock to find out people thought I was dead."

"So if you weren't dead, where have you been?"

He was supposed to say he'd been on hiatus, discovering his creative self. They'd thrashed out these questions for half the day yesterday, but as he sat there in the studio, none of the scripted answers were right. He couldn't lie to his fans, or his mates. If they'd read his text sent an hour ago, they were probably listening in.

"Rehab." In some respects, it was a bigger hell than actually being dead. Vince shook his head, his eyes wide at the revelation, but Riley ignored him. This had to be said.

"I've been completely sober for nearly eight years now…" Applause broke out and he glanced up to see Vince and the two hosts clapping. "Thank you. Being sober will be a lifelong challenge for me. One thing has helped me through, and that is my music."

"Well, this stunning news that Riley Le Breton is the new name for Riley Micah, ex-lead singer of pop band So You Think has blown up our text line. Greg from Bundaberg says My sister loved your music. She is going to lose it when she hears this. Oh, this one is a lot of excited swearwords and exclamation marks. So You Think didn't get much airtime on Triple J back in the day, but how about we play one of your old songs? What will it be?"

"Street Cry." Riley hadn't heard any of So You Think's stuff since the band broke up except for the occasional time in a shop when he couldn't avoid it. Street Cry had always been his favourite. The end of the second chorus was incredibly difficult to sing; he'd been so bloody proud of himself when he'd nailed it. As the tune came on, and the on air light went off, he leaned back in his chair.

"Holy shit. Riley Micah. This is the biggest news in music in a long time. You are back and your new tune is so amazing. It has the same upbeat style of So You Think but is much more mature and interesting."

"Hardly surprising now we know it's you."

What could you say to that? "Firstly I didn't write any of the So You Think songs, and yes, I'm a lot older and mature now." It was logic, that was all. If he hadn't fucked it all up, perhaps him and Ethan could have written their third album. They'd been playing around with ideas in the few quiet moments on the tour bus, whenever Riley wasn't off his head. What a waste of an opportunity. The memory grounded him.

"We are back with Riley Le Breton to talk about his new song and the staggering revelation that he is Riley Micah, the lead singer of pop band So You Think. And we have a rather interesting caller on the phone. Bella has called from the other side of the world; South London. She runs the website RMInHeaven, one of the many websites dedicated to the memory of Riley Micah. Hi Bella. It must be a shock to hear Riley's voice and discover he isn't dead."

"Riley. Riley. I love you. Marry me." The shrill excitement threw Riley back to his teen years. What had he done? It was too late to apologise and call it all a hoax. He'd told the world who he was and now he had to deal with the intense wild fans.

"Well, that was interesting. Is that what you expected when you decided to out yourself, Riley?"

He coughed to cover a laugh. "Ahhh, the So You Think fans were always quite vigorous in their adoration of the band, although I was not the prettiest one." He was the gayest one though. Their record company had been determined to keep that secret, and he'd already shocked everyone enough today. It'd been part of the contract he'd signed, that he'd only be seen in public with women. He was bisexual, and when he was eighteen he'd figured that would be easy enough to fulfil their conditions. The record company were about to offer him the world—or so he'd naively thought—

and besides their contract didn't cover private parties where anything and everything happened.

"That'd be Dylan."

The other host scoffed in a jovial way. "I always thought the two hottest members were you, and Ethan."

Riley grinned. "I think the most common ship was Ethan and Dylan." He'd fucked Dylan once at a party when they'd both been wasted; maybe he wasn't the gayest one, just the most comfortable with his sexuality back then. Ethan was the one who was the most wild in public and the most uptight in private. In their own ways, they were all putting on a show.

"We know that Ethan Nguyen has built a strong record as a songwriter since So You Think broke up. Are you all musically talented?"

Riley had had this question a zillion times during his So You Think days. "Being in a boy band takes more than a pretty face. They had over six thousand applicants for So You Think, so yes, we are all musically talented."

"And pretty." One of the hosts fluttered her eyelashes at him.

"It is awkward to think of myself like that. Being a teen idol was fine when I was a teen, but now it's a decade later, and I hope people will judge me on my music."

"Does that mean we will be hearing more from Riley Le Breton?"

Riley nodded. "Yes. I have brought along a new release today and I'm working on an album." He had enough material for a couple of albums, but he was still figuring out how he wanted to put them together. Some of the songs were too dark, written while he was in recovery. Those songs might never be heard by anyone else. Other songs were missing that elusive star quality that would make them into a proper pop song.

"Oh, an album. How about we play the new song and see what our listeners think? Maybe our text line will become more than incoherent excited squealing?"

Riley gritted his teeth. He hated the way people dismissed boy band fans as silly teenage girls. The misogyny dripped uncomfortably. "Being excited about something shouldn't be dismissed as unimportant. I always loved the excitement and joy that So You Think fans brought to our concerts. It is no fault of theirs that the band had issues."

"Issues that led to rehab for you?"

"That's rather an oversimplification. So You Think had some messy contractual issues with our record label—issues that have been widely discussed in the media—and I think it's fair to say that the pressure surrounding those problems was partially to blame for the fall of So You Think. My personal problems were exacerbated by the collapse of the band." He'd long ago learned not to blame the band for that whole blurry mess. "I'm not ashamed of my past, and I take full responsibility for my role in how So You Think ended. It was a complex situation and yes, I have plenty of regrets. It's just that I'd rather talk about my new songs and see what your listeners think."

The host nodded. "Well said. Here it is, brand new music from Riley Le Breton. You heard it here first, So You Think's lead singer Riley Micah has rebranded as a solo artist and now we have a global premier of his new tune, Authentic." She pushed the button and the song started playing. The on air light went off, and Riley eased out a long breath. It didn't calm the tremble in his stomach.

"I think that's enough for today." Vince stood abruptly and reached out with his hand for the hosts to shake. "Thank you so much for having Riley on your show."

"It's been a pleasure."

"I'm not a fan of the surprise. Next time just give us a confidential heads up."

"I'm sorry." Riley adjusted his hat. "That was my idea. I wanted to know if I would be recognised. Sorry."

"It's okay. We can deal with a little drama for the morning, and we get to be the ones who told the world, so all is forgiven. Come back when you ready to drop your album."

"Will do." Vince pushed open the door and Riley waltzed out. Thank fuck that was over; except he knew it was only the beginning... There would be many more interviews now.

4

Vince was glad Riley didn't try and engage him in conversation as they walked through the building back to the underground carpark. From the moment Riley had gone off script, Vince's ears had filled with a roaring noise. They had a script for a reason; they'd spent hours figuring out how to best tell Riley's story for the greatest financial gain, and he'd just casually thrown in a grenade with no discussion about how that might blow up the media. Despite what people said, not all press was good press, and he'd wanted to build on Riley's pop persona. Talking about rehab was too dark for the image. Every step towards the basement vibrated through Vince's chest, and now they were alone in the dimly lit carpark, Vince turned to glare at his client.

"Rehab? Rehab?" Vince could have throttled his client. It wasn't just that Riley had thrown him a curveball… Vince would never have taken a drunkard on as a client. He had rules against that kind of thing, for a good fucking reason.

"Is that a problem? I've been sober for eight years. I don't care who you are, but in my book, that's one heck of an achievement."

"Says the man who didn't disclose he'd been in rehab when we signed an agreement."

Riley growled. "The contract we signed said I had to disclose any current personal issues that might affect my ability to do my part of the deal. I shouldn't have to talk about going to rehab unless I choose to. It was a long time ago."

"But you did disclose it. You went off script." The pressure on Vince's skull tightened to the point of explosion.

"Fine. I should have told you, but I was embarrassed. Okay."

Vince clenched and unclenched his fist. "Not too embarrassed to tell the fucking world."

"I realised I couldn't lie to all my fans. They deserve to know the truth."

"The truth." Vince spluttered out a laugh. It was either that or strangle Riley. Or kiss him. The air crackled between them. With rage or something else? Sheer energy, and he wanted to drink it all in, suck this chemistry down into his lungs where he could use it to fuel his life force. "I want all of the truth right now, because your embarrassment can get fucked."

Riley lifted his chin a little and Vince's stomach sank. He shouldn't have asked. What if the truth was something he couldn't deal with? What else was he going to reveal? Damn it was hot in this carpark, stifling. His clothes felt sticky against his skin and he wanted to peel them off.

"You are asking for a lot. How do I know it's safe to tell you everything? I mean, look at you and your angry face."

"Huh?" Vince didn't like this. He really didn't need a high maintenance client like Riley was proving to be. Vince sucked in a quick breath—he was lying to himself—Riley wasn't emotionally difficult. He was so fucking sexy with his clear amber brown eyes and his cocky self-assurance.

Vince practically vibrated with unleashed tension. "It's my job to manage how the world sees you. I can't do that without all the information."

"Fine. You want to know everything. Here is the everything." Riley stood with his hands on his hips and it took all of Vince's concentration not to stare at Riley's hands and the way his shirt pulled tight over his abdomen.

"When I first signed with So You Think, we had to agree to being straight in public. I nearly didn't sign, because that's pretty fucked up, but I was young and hungry for the opportunity."

The roar in Vince's ears changed to a hum. "Straight in public. What the fuck?" He breathed in sharply. "Does that mean you are gay?" Even to himself that sounded like an accusation, when the truth—Vince's truth—was that little snippet of information made lust run in his veins like a wild horse galloping over broad pastures.

"Bisexual if you must know. And there you have it. All the fucking truths that you are so keen to know. Am I too much of a liability for you now?"

Vince had never been tempted to fuck a client before, so he'd never had to worry about that particular ethical dilemma until now. Temptation circled, soared like an eagle waiting to swoop on its prey. Was it really such a big deal if they both consented? Riley sniffed and Vince realised he'd been quiet for too long and there was only conclusion Riley could draw from that. He probably assumed Vince was a bigot. He'd hardly guess at the truth, would he? Vince was so fucking attracted to Riley that his legs had turned to lead and he couldn't move. There was really only one way to deal with Riley's revelation, the assumption Vince could see in Riley's hooded stare, and the chemistry crackling in the air around them. Vince took two decisive steps forward, wrapped one hand around the back of Riley's neck, and kissed him. Insta-lust turned into instant combustion. The world around disappeared, and only their lips existed. Riley kissed him back, a conversation of need and lust and heat with a hint of coffee and mint.

"Wait." Riley pushed Vince on the chest. Vince took a step back, panting for air. The kiss had robbed him of breath, just whisked it away on a stolen moment and he yearned for more. A tiny voice in the back of his brain tried to scream that Riley was an addict, and Vince knew exactly how a relationship with an addict would end, but the other noises inside him—his beating heart, his raspy breath, the wind in his ears—were too loud. He wanted more. Desperately.

"Wow. Um, I guess that answers the question on how you feel about me being bisexual, but don't you have a…" Riley pressed his fingers to the bridge of his nose.

"A what?" Vince's brain felt like scrambled eggs.

"You know. A thing about clients and stuff?"

He hauled in a deep breath. "Ethically, I probably

shouldn't kiss a client, no, but there is nothing legal to prevent it. Ethics is all about power balance." And right now, Riley had all the power, or at least, that's how it felt, and no, he wasn't about to think too hard about why that was uncomfortable. He wanted to squirm, or fight for control. Right; that went some way to explaining the riot in his gut. Vince needed to control his life; no wonder his stomach flipped over at the idea of gifting some of that control to someone else.

"I don't understand you."

"What do you mean?" With anyone else, Vince would have said that he was a simple man. He wanted success and money. He was good at knowing what motivated people to spend money and he'd built a whole damned business around it.

"You can't just kiss me in a goddamned basement right after scolding me for not considering the public's response to rehab."

The muscles in Vince's neck tightened. "Your disclosure of rehab without warning is a lot different to a private kiss."

"Do you regret kissing me?" Riley's cheeks had heightened colour on them, a patchy redness that made his black hair and faint stubble sharper.

"Never." The too brief kiss had been the hottest kiss he'd ever had. With an apparently sober addict. Fuck. What had he been thinking? He wiped his clammy palms on his jeans. He hadn't been thinking, not with his brain, anyway. "I don't like it when a client goes off script and reveals information like that." It was true, although it didn't touch on why

Vince was wary of addicts, even sober ones. He wouldn't go there. "I wish we'd planned it."

Riley's eyes narrowed a tiny amount. "That makes sense."

"What?"

"Nothing."

"That look isn't nothing." Vince cursed his big mouth. He shouldn't be so bloody curious about the way Riley looked at him.

Riley held up one hand. "I think I need a bit of space for a while."

"Because I kissed you?"

"Because it's a terrible idea to make a decision in a place of heightened stress."

Vince staggered back a step as if Riley had hit him. A sucker punch in the ribcage. "I stress you?"

"It's not you. I've just had my first press interview in nearly a decade. I need space to process everything." For the first time since Vince had met Riley, his voice wasn't clear and strong. Vince breathed in. Advertising was all about people management. This wasn't about him, even if that kiss had been intimately personal.

"Get in the car. I'll drive you to your place." If Riley wanted space, Vince would give it to him. He pulled out his keys, pushed the button, and slid into the front seat of his car. He plugged his phone in. Shit. A zillion notifications. He flicked his thumb over them, quickly reading and processing the news—mostly his staff notifying him of the reactions to Riley's interview—and waited for Riley to join him. Eventually, the door clicked shut.

"Thanks for that. I've decided what I want."

Vince looked up from his phone. "Okay?" He pressed his heels against the car floor so his leg wouldn't jiggle with impatience. The completely unsurprising news that Riley had made global headlines wasn't going to change in the next few minutes. Riley Micah's return from apparent death was the biggest news in the music industry for years.

"I think we should have sex."

Vince spluttered out a hard cough. "Excuse me?" That wasn't what Vince had expected at all. His cock hardened at the idea, so obviously his body had no qualms about this plan.

"There's obviously chemistry between us, and if this whole announcement goes to plan—"

Vince bit his tongue. He wasn't going to interrupt to tell Riley the plan was flying to instant viral success because this was going somewhere much more intimate and fascinating.

"—well, we will be needing to work together quite closely." Riley hesitated for a fraction of a second. "I think we should get it out of our system now."

"Hold on. You think we should have sex because that will get rid of this inconvenient chemistry between us." Vince tried his damnedest not to sound incredulous.

"Yes." Riley sounded so certain that his wild plan would work.

"Sure. I mean I'm hardly going to turn you down after that kiss." Vince didn't think he'd get bored with Riley any time soon, but he was hardly going to cock-block himself. "My place?"

Riley coughed. "Now?"

Vince shrugged. "Well, you see, your little announcement has made global news. So it's either sex now while we have a short window when no one will expect a response, or we go to the Kapow offices and start scheduling interviews."

"Oh. Umm. Now is good, I guess."

Vince's body screamed in protest at having pleasure taken away before he'd gotten anything. "Don't tell me you were bluffing."

"I wasn't bluffing. I just thought we could, you know, have dinner first or something." Damn, Riley wanted to be wooed with his own proposal. If that kiss hadn't been so flammable, he might have been able to pretend Riley's idea wasn't that big a deal.

"According to you, we need to get this done and out of the way so that we can work together without being distracted. In case you've forgotten it's early in the morning. I dragged myself out of bed early to go to work for you and be there for your breakfast show interview. Let's go to bed now, sort out your little scheme, and be back at work by lunchtime." *Yeah, sure Vince.* He wanted to roll his eyes at himself; as if this was all a pragmatic matter that could be resolved before lunch. Any other day he'd say that he hadn't had enough coffee for this; except that kiss had his neurons firing faster than a caffeine hit.

Riley's face blazed with colour. "I was rather hoping you'd dedicate a little more time to this. You know, to properly get rid of—"

"All this pesky chemistry? How long do you think it will take?" Months and fucking months, if Vince had his way. Hell, he could probably kiss Riley for hours without doing much else. Just to absorb the entire experience.

"I mean, it's either going to be awkward and we won't do it at all. Or once won't be enough."

Vince closed his eyes. "Can you listen to yourself? You want to fuck me out of your system, but once won't be enough? Which one is it going to be?"

"I don't know. I just know I can't concentrate on work after that kiss."

"What about this one?" Vince leaned across and brushed his lips over Riley's mouth. Desire flashed down his spine and if he wasn't squashed into his car, he'd be all over Riley.

"Just drive. We can work out the rest later." The rough edge to Riley's voice sent a fresh shiver over Vince's skin. He turned the car on and revved the engine.

"Hold on." This was going to a quick ride home; through all the back streets and rat runs to avoid traffic. And to think, this morning, he'd contemplated walking across Pyrmont Bridge to the studio. That would've been a grave miscalculation!

5

One of the ways Riley had learned to stay sober was to ensure he didn't get into highly emotional situations. He'd broken nearly all his rules today—deliberately. Just over a week ago, he'd stood on the porch of his share house in Bourke and realised he couldn't say yes to the office job he'd been offered. He couldn't spend the rest of his life in Bourke, while Riley Le Breton took off online. But if he was to be a musician full time again, it involved taking a massive risk. Everything he'd worked so hard for—sobriety, a sense of self, friendship—would be difficult to maintain. He'd need to find a way to keep those in a place of importance. The initial battle for sobriety had difficult; and he wasn't sure he could go through withdrawals again. The odds were against him; always had been. Nearly eighty percent of addicts fell off the wagon. That he hadn't—yet—was special and he didn't want to ruin that.

Vince had given him the perfect way to get rid of all this nervous energy surging in his body. The post interview adrenalin needed to be dealt with, one way or another. He would not, could not, have a drink to settle himself, even though he could taste the sharp dryness of gin on his tongue. Or was that the taste of Vince's kiss? Vince seemed to buy his 'get it out of our system' excuse, and now his expensive sports car hugged the road as Vince threaded it through traffic towards a bed. Any bed would do. Riley probably should care where they were going.

"Where are you taking me?"

"My place. Is that alright? It's private."

Riley swallowed. "How private? I don't want anyone to see me." Not after that interview. The whole world's music media would likely be talking about him, and he wanted to control their first images of him.

"Better than a hotel, mate. Underground carpark, private elevator, no one will see you."

Riley glanced sideways at Vince whose hands gripped the steering wheel tight. "Private elevator?"

"One of the perks of having money." Vince phrased that as if he knew what it was like to not have money. Riley shouldn't care, shouldn't be interested in him as a person. He only wanted his body and the release it promised. Vince drove the car into a driveway underneath a high rise building and leaned out the window to swipe his card. The boom rose up and Vince drove into the carpark, eventually parking around the corner in a hidden nook. "Here we go."

Riley leaped out of the car, his heart still thumping quickly, then slammed to a stop as he spun around to see a familiar vehicle. "That's my ute."

"Yeah, Kapow has offices on the first two floors, and I live in the penthouse."

"You said no one would see us."

Vince pointed to a set of two elevators on the far side of the parking garage. "Only the people who work in this building. They use those elevators. Mine is here." A metallic door was tucked behind Vince's car. Vince walked over to it and waved his swipe card. The doors opened and Riley followed Vince inside. The lift had five buttons, three with names on, one for a gym, and one that said Ground Floor.

"You said it was private." The doors closed behind him; the ground floor button bothered him the most, anyone could open those doors. His chest heaved as his pulse worked overtime. He wasn't ready for the paparazzi yet and he had way too much leftover bounce from this morning's interview. People had loved his new song—that thrill would never get old!

"It is. The doors only open with a swipe card and the other two residents who have their own level will be at work right now."

"So private doesn't mean just for you, it—"

Vince grinned. "Mate, this is as private as you'll get in the city." He pressed the button with his name beside it, and the lift whooshed up so fast it left Riley's stomach behind. He sucked in a short breath; doubt could flee because he was alone with Vince in an elevator away from the media. Riley wasn't here to fuck spiders, although the intense expression on Vince's face reminded him of the way a Huntsman stared before he pounced. He wasn't going to leave this move to Vince. Riley would be the hunter. He might be an inch

38

shorter than Vince, but he'd worked on a road crew for the past eight years. He had to be stronger, and with two long strides he proved it. He placed his hands on Vince's chest and pressed him up against the lift wall. Vince didn't protest, only parted his lips in what could only be an invitation.

"Yes." Riley kissed Vince. Taste and texture exploded on his tongue in a hot rush of need. Vince wrapped his arms around Riley's waist, pulling him closer, and Riley pushed his knee between Vince's legs. Oh hell, he was going to swoon. Vince's cock rubbed against him, a hard solid length, and Riley lost the ability to think. A ding interrupted their kiss.

"We are here. Welcome to my house." Vince pushed against him, chest to chest, then took his hands off Riley's waist, and walked out of the elevator. Riley panted for breath, then staggered after him. His blood surged through his veins, pulsing with heat. The jittery adrenalin from this morning's interview and the way Vince had argued with him afterwards, and every word they'd exchanged since, all combined into a wild needy fire. Vince stood in a small foyer and waved his card beside a double width door. It'd been years since Riley had been in such luxurious surroundings. Music executives and rich people loved to have So You Think as guests at their parties. His breath hitched at the memory. He was an indie artist now, he didn't need to do what the record label wanted.

"Come in." Vince glanced over his shoulder and the fragment of a smile was enough to banish the past. Riley aimed for a casual walk, a strut, but nearly tripped over his own damned feet in his rush to go with Vince. He was about to break his sex drought. He probably couldn't have someone better than Vince who had an incredible body, kissed like a champion, and had the aura of a man who knew exactly what he wanted from life. Vince exuded confidence and that made him handsome, even though he wasn't classically proportioned.

Riley had barely made it inside, when the door closed with a quiet snick, and Vince pushed him up against it. Vince's hard body was broad and muscular—built in a gym for perfection—and there for Riley's exploration. Before he could run his hands up Vince's spine, he was being thoroughly kissed and he opened his mouth for more. Vince's groan vibrated on his tongue, and he drank it in. More. He needed more. They tussled, desperate to taste each other, all lips and tongue and teeth. The bitter notes of coffee with an aftertaste of mint, and that bloody hint of gin again. If Riley couldn't have the real thing, he could have it in Vince's kiss. A little danger sign clanged at the back of his skull but he shoved it aside. Right now, he needed release— one that he wasn't addicted to—and Vince was here with his seductive kiss and busy hands. He placed his hands on Vince's lower back, right as Vince tilted his hips and rubbed his cock against Riley's own. Heat shot through his body.

"Fucking hell, Vince."

"Too much?"

Riley pressed a kiss to Vince's neck, on the edge of his stubble. The rough texture against his lips was exactly what he wanted. "Too many clothes." He tugged Vince's shirt and it slid out of the waistband of his suit pants. The expensive linen shirt was cool in his hands, a contrast to the heat of Vince's skin.

"Fuck yeah." Vince's hands pulled at Riley's t-shirt. He'd worn a plain green one for today's interview; Kapow had decided on a look for Riley Le Breton that was a grown up version of Riley Micah—tight jeans, plain t-shirt, dark brown leather jacket. They'd all agonised over his outfit for hours, and now Vince made short work of removing it all. The jacket dropped off his arms, ending up squished between Riley's spine and the door. Riley's fingers fumbled on the buttons of Vince's shirt.

"Lift up your arms." Vince's command whispered hoarsely over Riley's mouth and he gave up on Vince's shirt. He slid his hands up Vince's sides, over his ribs, and then lifted his arms above his head. His leather jacket fell to the floor, as Vince hooked one arm around Riley's waist, and with the other, he threaded the t-shirt up Riley's body, over his face, and up his arms until he stood naked from the waist up. Vince's gaze roamed freely over Riley, leaving a heated trail as if he'd touched him, and he shivered. Ready for his touch.

"You still have it." Vince croaked. He still had what? But then Vince bent his head and sucked Riley's nipple ring and he remembered on a deep groan. He'd always had sensitive nipples and loved having them played with. His head hit the back of the door with a soft thud. OMG. Vince flicked the ring back and forth with his tongue, then gripped it with his teeth and gave a little tug that shot heat direct to Riley's cock.

"You knew?" Riley managed to summon a word or two

between the pulses of pleasure from Vince's tongue and teeth.

Vince shifted to rest his chin on the nipple ring. "We had to sort through a lot of old photos of you for your website."

"Right." Of course; there were no secrets in the music industry. "Oh fuck me." A hazy memory prickled at the edges.

"Is there a problem?"

Riley wasn't sure if he wanted to laugh or grimace. "Yeah. As my PR person, you probably need to know that there's likely a photo of me out there getting a..." Technically it wasn't a dick tattoo as it went around the base of it. "Groin tattoo." He'd had it done at a penthouse similar to this, but in Monte Carlo. A drugged up dare. Fucking Ethan standing over him at a party, yelling 'I got one, you should too.' He vaguely remembered saying he didn't want it anywhere someone could see, and Ethan had suggested the location. They'd all laughed, as if it was the biggest fucking joke, while a professional tattoo artist shaved his pubes and prepped him for it. At least a pro had done it.

"Now that I need to see."

"The photo?"

Vince shrugged. "No. The tattoo. Does it say anything?"

"No." And thank fuck for that; God knows what words he might have had written on himself while out of it. "It's the music for our biggest hit, Weekend Hustler." Riley stepped out of Vince's embrace and pulled down his jeans. Peeled them off, more like. He'd wanted to go for a looser look—he was too damned old for this trendy bullshit—but

42

Kapow had overruled him. Eventually he kicked off his shoes and won the battle over tight denim. Vince pounced, cat like, and Riley gasped as skin collided with skin. While he'd been arguing with his jeans, Vince had stripped and now he rubbed his glorious hair covered pecs against Riley's bare chest. Their hands tangled in a rush to take Riley's undies off, and Vince slid downwards with them until he knelt in front of Riley.

"Beautiful." Vince's tongue hovered across his bottom lip as his gaze locked onto Riley's cock.

"The tattoo? It's alright."

Vince cleared his throat. "Not the tatt. Can I touch?"

"Yes." It came out as a needy whisper, a breathy almost moan, and when Vince flicked his tongue over the end of Riley's cock, the moan deepened. Riley was glad there was a door to lean against because blood rushed to his already hard cock and he needed something solid to support his legs. Vince traced the tattoo, his fingers lazily running around the base of Riley's cock. Holy fuck. If Vince put his mouth on him, he wasn't going to last long. He placed his hands on Vince's broad shoulders.

"Do you want this?"

"This being a blowjob? Yes, please."

Vince chuckled, his breath scattering warmth over Riley's cock. Hell. "So polite." Vince slid his mouth over Riley's cock. Heaven. Hot wet heaven and it took everything to grip onto Vince and not thrust wildly into Vince's mouth. Vince flattened his tongue and sucked him deep.

"Oh God. Fuck. Fucking fuck. That's incredible." He was babbling nonsense but he didn't care. Vince's tight mouth moved on him, slippery and hot, teasing him until Riley's balls tightened up and he nearly came. He stroked Vince's cheek, and pressed his thumb to the edge of his mouth.

"Stop."

Vince slid off and Riley immediately regretted asking.

"I mean. I'm going to come, so maybe…"

"You can if you need."

"Not yet." He used his thumb to tug gently at the corner of Vince's mouth. "Come here." Vince rose up and kissed him. Bloody hell. The kiss had a new edge to it, the salty taste of pre-cum, and Riley's hips rocked against Vince. Vince wrapped his hand around both their cocks, cleverly deepening the kiss while he stroked them both. Riley tilted his head, ready to explode. He ran his hand down Vince's spine, across all those glorious muscles, and gripped his arse. Tight. Vince groaned into his mouth, and when Riley sucked his tongue, their moans mingled together. Riley couldn't hold on anymore. Vince had shredded his control. Riley clung onto him, one hand on Vince's arse, the other on the back of his neck, and he kissed him as if the world was ending. Perhaps it was; judging by the way his body trembled with heat and need, flashing through his veins, until he came in Vince's hand. Vince joined him, thrusting together, their cocks rubbing between their bodies, slick with come. His body vibrated as if a series of bass notes beat loudly through a subwoofer.

"Fuck me, that was incredible."

Vince kissed him on the forehead. "Yes. And yes, I'll fuck you again. In a moment."

"How can you even talk?" Riley wanted to lie down and snooze. All the tension from the morning's interview, the nerves, the adrenalin, the post-interview shakes, it had all spilled out onto Vince's taut abdominal muscles. He'd wanted release and boy oh boy had he gotten more than he'd needed.

"Gah." Vince laughed, then grabbed Riley's hand in a gesture that was far too intimate and pulled him through the open plan lounge towards a long leather couch. "Sit down."

Riley hesitated. He didn't want to smear the couch with semen.

"It's fine. The cleaners will sort it."

"Perhaps a paper towel or something first." Riley had looked after himself for long enough now that he wasn't going to make extra work for someone, even if they were paid to deal with his mess.

"Sure. Or you are welcome to use the shower."

Riley's feet were heavy. If he had a shower, he'd probably drown himself. "Maybe later." What he needed now was rest. His body felt emptied out and hollow. Spying a blanket, he threw it on the leather and collapsed in a heap.

"You okay?"

"Very tired." His eyes closed almost as soon as his head hit the couch, and his limbs went slack. He let out a long breath. This was exactly what he needed. A way to release tension after a performance that wasn't one of his old drugs of choice. The little bell in the back of skull tinkled gently—don't let Vince become a replacement habit—before sleep claimed him.

6

An hour later, Vince took the lift down the foyer to collect the food he'd ordered. Riley had been so cute asleep on his couch with his hair all tussled and his limbs in disarray. He'd emitted little snores as Vince had cleaned him up, then covered him with another blanket. And if Riley couldn't get any more gorgeous—cute was the wrong word for a thirty year old bloke—he'd snuggle into the second blanket with a deep sigh. Damn. Vince had been right. Once was not going to be enough to get this man out of his system. Riley had this creative unabandoned streak that was so appealing because it was so free. Free from judgement and the weight of the world that came with it. A week ago, Vince would've told anyone that he couldn't stand the upbeat pop of So You Think, that he'd thump a wall if anyone dared play that bloody CD near him. Now... Now he wasn't so sure. He'd been sucked into the world of Riley, especially with his new Riley Le Breton songs which had a maturity to go with the happy escapism.

"Lunch is here." He placed the plastic containers with various Thai dishes from a local restaurant on the coffee table and opened them up. Fresh herbs, chilli, and other mouth watering aromas filled the air. Riley cracked open one eye, then slowly sat up and rolled his neck on his shoulders. The blanket fell off and landed in his lap, unfortunately covering his beautiful cock and hilarious tattoo. There had to be story about that, especially if Riley was worried there were photos somewhere.

"You didn't have to do that."

Vince shrugged. "You are my guest. Of course, I'm going to feed you. Anyway, I know it's a bit early for lunch, but I was starving after getting up early—"

"And exercising." Riley winked.

"Yeah, that. And we need to head down to work soon."

"Thanks. I haven't had Thai in forever." He leaned forward and grabbed some chopsticks. Vince probably shouldn't ask. They were supposed to be getting this out of their systems so they could work together. Being curious wasn't part of the plan.

"So a dick tattoo, and with photos of it; that's very rock star."

Riley blushed a little and picked up a prawn with his chopsticks. "Yeah, I guess. Wild times, back then."

"I thought I'd heard of most things, you know being in advertising we see a lot of shit, but…"

"You really want to know about this? Do you think people will go a bit silly if that photo gets out into the world?"

Vince should've pounced on the excuse to make it about

work. "I was more curious for myself." Fuck. Why did he say that?

"Ha. It was at a party in Monte Carlo. I don't even remember who was there or why we were invited… Anyway they had a tattoo artist there, at the party. Ethan got a rose or some shit added to his sleeve and everyone said I should get one. I was supposed to be the clean looking one, so they all joked about where I could get it done where no one could see. I said I didn't want one on my arse—I wanted to be able to see it myself. Anyway, long story short, we'd all done a fuck ton of coke and I woke up with a tattoo around the base of my dick and a text message from some random number saying they had a photo of it and did I want it."

"I should represent more rock stars! That sounds…" Vince ought to say fun because that was what people said, but he'd grown up around that shit and part of him—the logical part—regretted taking Riley on as a client. He didn't want to be exposed to all this; ironic really given that he worked in advertising. But then, he'd always had a good instinct for money and when people weren't sober, they told him useful things. The little flutter of guilt was easy to push away because it wasn't a typical response to his self-evaluation.

Riley grimaced and stabbed the rice with his chopsticks. "Yeah, nah. I hate not remembering it all. That party was kind of the beginning of the end. So You Think was at the top of the charts and everyone wanted us, but we had no money and there was all this pressure to perform as if we had mega wealth. The only people making money out of us were the record label."

"That's crap."

"Yeah. Thankfully the three of us stuck together as much as we could, but then Dylan started writing songs for the record label and I was never sober, and Ethan met his first wife and it all went off the rails."

Vince mulled that over for a moment. "You and Ethan thought Dylan had sold out?"

"Good guess. And I guess we dealt with it in our own fucked up ways. One day I woke up in a rehab facility with no idea how I'd got there, and realised that I wasn't ready to die."

"Fucking hell." The parallel to Vince's father was far too raw. He'd been the one to drop his dad off at rehab, over and over, but the arsehole had always left before finishing the treatment. Vince bit the inside of his mouth. He wasn't going to ask how many times Riley had gone through rehab before he had decided he was sober. What the fuck was he doing? He knew how this ended. Addicts didn't change their habits.

"It took years before the three of us spoke again. Ethan's second wife is the daughter of one of the record label executives, and he works for them now. He's very much the buttoned up clean accountant type now."

"Eat up. Let's go to work." Vince focused on his lunch. It was excellent, crisp vegetables stir fried with plenty of heat and flavour. Once they'd finished up, he collected all the plastic containers and threw them in the sink.

"One other thing." Riley stood up and wrapped the blanket around his waist. He looked like a fucking Scottish highlander or something with the plaid print flowing off his naked hips. Vince swallowed.

"Yeah?"

"I don't want any parties. I can't do that old pop star stuff anymore. I'm too… old."

Vince ran his tongue across the back of his teeth. Why had Riley hesitated?

"Anything you want. You're the client." He needed to push him back into that space. "Let's go."

Riley nodded. "Thanks, and hey thanks for lunch too." He grabbed his clothes from the chair. "Did you put these here?"

"Is that a problem?"

"Nah, all good, mate. I'm sorry for crashing like that."

Vince was caught between kissing Riley to reassure him everything was cool, and pushing him out of his house, because he really didn't need the type of mess that Riley was going to bring into his life. "No problem."

"Okay?" Riley ran his hand through his hair.

"You don't have to look like a fucking scared rabbit. I care for those who—"

"—you fuck? Cool. Whatever."

Vince's grandparents had ingrained it in him, to care for those who matter to him. "Sure. Let's call it that." He wasn't about to admit that he'd nearly said he might be starting to care for Riley. Who was the fucking mess now? He was. He wanted to get rid of Riley the addict, and he wanted to keep Riley the fucking sexy naked guy who was casually pulling on his jeans in the middle of his lounge. He pulled the green t-shirt over his head—so hot—and glanced up at Vince.

When did putting on clothes send a shiver of desire racing up his spine? Vince had lost it. To even entertain the concept of Riley the addict should have had him bolting like the bunny he'd just accused Riley of being. Well, it was the wide eyed look that had spurred that comment.

"Hey, I'll clean up the lunch dishes if you want."

"It's takeaway, plus the cleaner will sort it. She likes to wash the plastic and reuse it for her kid's lunchboxes." Shut it, Vince. Damn he never babbled like this. His employees at Kapow would all say that he was a gruff man of few words; just the necessary ones, and here he was volunteering pointless information.

"Hey. That's neat. I like that idea."

"Yeah. You ready?" Vince grabbed his swipe card and marched to the door. He held it open and Riley brushed past his shoulder on his way out. Vince shut down the shiver. All Riley had wanted was sex to get it out his system. His easy touch was a fucking earthquake of a tremor across Vince's skin and he knew that this wouldn't be the last time he invited Riley up here. He stepped into the lift and crossed his arms.

"You okay?"

"Yip." Vince had a new plan. Pass Riley over to his staff as soon as they stepped into the office and hunker down in his own office to focus on running Kapow.

"Okay then." Riley's jaw stiffened, that little muscle at the bottom corner taut.

Vince squared his shoulders. "We need to get to work. My phone has blown up with messages from my staff about your interview. There are requests for more media. We—"

"I know. Look, I suggested we do this. If it's awkward for you now, I'm sorry. I'll keep my distance."

The lift doors opened and Vince shrugged rather than answer. "I'm good. Let's just get to work."

Riley grabbed him by the shoulders and pushed him back against the wall of the elevator. "I don't believe you. Something happened while I was asleep, didn't it?"

"No." Vince stared into Riley's brown eyes, into the deep raging emotion. "Fine. There is something, but it's… I can't talk about it now."

Riley pressed the door closed button. "Yes you can. I won't work with someone who can't talk about things."

"Says the fucking addict." Vince closed his eyes. Shit. Fuck and blast.

"Ahhh. Now we have the truth. You shouted at me for not disclosing rehab, and you've been weird ever since I mentioned my tattoo. You—" Riley poked him in the chest. "You have a problem with me and my past."

"Yes."

"Want to talk about it?"

"No."

Riley tilted his head to the side and gave Vince a look that he couldn't interpret. "Huh. I didn't pick you for a reformed addict."

"I'm not."

"A family member?"

Vince growled. "What part of I don't want to talk about it, don't you understand?"

Riley's mouth curled up at one edge and Vince wanted to kiss the slyness right off his face.

"Definitely a family member then. Hell, I'm sorry. I should have told you."

"Yes, you should have." Vince's pulse skyrocketed. Was it the topic or the way Riley still had his hands pressed on Vince's pecs? The latter, surely.

"Let's go to work and I'll tell the whole sordid tale to everyone, so they know how to spin it. The world is going to want to know and we can sell—"

For the first time in ages, Vince smiled properly. "Yes. We can sell an exclusive interview." He held Riley's wrists and plucked his hands off his own chest, then dropped Riley's hand so he could press the open button and get to work.

"Truce?"

"If it matters to you, then yes."

Riley leaned closer and his lips brushed against Vince's ear. Heat shot down his spine, direct to his dick. He was in so much trouble.

"It matters. Just like your kisses matter to me. Next time…"

Vince swallowed. "There might not be a next time."

"Not if I have anything to say about it."

The doors opened and Vince marched away. He twisted to look over his shoulder. Bloody Riley stood there with one hip cocked and one eyebrow raised, and Vince almost forgot he was in the foyer of his workplace.

7

R iley had forgotten this about the music world. Everything happened at lightning speed. Driving a grader along a dirt road out the back of Bourke occurred at a much slower pace, one he'd grown comfortable with.

"Are you ready for your interview?" Uma asked. She was one of many people who worked at Kapow and had been dealing with his situation.

"Yes. And hey, thanks for everything."

Uma smiled, her dark brown eyes lighting up. "It's no problem. You are the most exciting project I've dealt with in ages. Kapow has dragged everyone off their usual work to deal with this week."

"Right." He didn't really need the reminder that he was paying all these people to create publicity plans for him.

"Muhit ran the data overnight for you, and your web hits have been massive. Your socials are viral, and your new song hit number one on three different streaming channels."

Riley's body buzzed with the news. "Sweet. That's really

great." At least he'd be able to pay Kapow for everything they'd done now. He scoffed under his breath. It wasn't relief that caused this fizz in his veins, it was unmitigated excitement. The money would be good and the risks he'd taken to engage Kapow would pay off, but ultimately, what truly made his heart leap was knowing people loved his music. So much had happened since his revelation on breakfast radio, he could barely believe that was only yesterday. Vince had been nowhere to be seen since they'd arrived back at Kapow. He'd handed Riley over to a group of people, then disappeared. Riley had been too busy to examine how that had made him feel. The reality was that he shouldn't care; he'd used him for sexual release, they'd discussed it up front, and the deal was over. If only it didn't nag at him, somewhere in the dim recesses of his mind.

Craig walked into the room and Riley tried not to show his distaste. Something about the slick looking man made his skin crawl, although he hadn't really given him a reason for the reaction. Instinct. Craig reminded him of some of the worst executives at his old record label. It wasn't really fair to Craig to paint him with the same brush when Riley had barely met him.

"Ready?"

"Yes." If people could stop asking that same bloody question, that would help too.

"No surprises today. Only what we've practiced." The abrupt reminder was probably what Riley needed but he didn't like the sneer that went with it, as if Craig looked down on him for something. Given the way the beers had flowed around the office last night, it was likely because

Riley had refused a drink then left. Being sober was nothing to be ashamed of. It'd been a hard fought battle and he'd rather head to his hotel room than stand around awkwardly refusing drinks all night. Besides, he knew from experience, he couldn't let himself be in that environment. It was too tempting. Vince had made no appearance at the after work drinks either.

"Sure." He attempted to sound light-hearted, but from the way Uma gave him a little side eye, he figured he hadn't succeeded. Whatever. This was his career, his goal. One slimy executive couldn't take that away from him. Not this time around the block. The door opened again, but Riley's sigh at yet another interruption caught in his mouth. Vince. Riley forgot everything—how to breathe, why he was here, the beat to his own songs—except his heart pulsed in the needy rhythm of Machine Gun Tom. Ratta tat tat boom boom, then that little trill of electronica. Vince scanned the room with a glance that would've been lazy on anyone else, but the intensity made the hairs on Riley's arms rise up. Nothing would get missed in Vince's observations.

"You ready?"

Riley forced a grin, even though what he really wanted was to bound up to Vince and kiss him until they both struggled for oxygen. "Not you too!"

"What?" A tiny furrow appeared between Vince's eyebrows.

"Yes, I'm ready." Focus, Riley, focus. He dragged a deep breath in through his nostrils and ended up with a lung full of five different eau d'perfumes. It must be his imagination since Vince stood leaning against the door frame, but he would swear he inhaled that hint of gin and salt that infused his kisses with Vince. No, not gin. Juniper berries. They were a much safer way to think of the scent except Riley had no clue of what they looked like or whatever.

"You sure?" Vince's incredulous tone dragged him back to the room.

"Yes. I've only been asked that by everyone under the fucking sun."

"How tedious of us. I will remind Anna to make a note for our next team meeting." He pulled out his phone and toyed with it. Riley stared at Vince, unable to work out if he jested or not.

"Um, okay?"

"I take it you've been thoroughly briefed, and you talked to your old band like we discussed?"

Riley nodded. After a long afternoon at Kapow going through all the media offers and trying to figure out which ones to accept and in which order, Riley had gone back to his hotel room to hide from the Kapow office drinks. He'd chatted to a few mates back in Bourke, and had apologised fuck knows how many times for using his middle name with them and pretending to be his own cousin. They'd all told him they'd guessed anyway, but plenty of people came to Bourke to hide and if he wanted to be Paul, then whatever, mate. It was going to a long running joke in the town at this rate. Then, as requested, he'd set up a video conference call with Dylan and Ethan. They weren't surprised by the media frenzy, and he was glad he'd told them his plans before embarking on this journey. Ethan's kids had jumped up and down in the back of the call, and their excitement was contagious. Shouts of "Uncle Riley" always helped him find a smile or two and were a little reminder of his own redemption. He couldn't fuck up his life again because he'd found joy in all the human moments of living.

"Yeah. It was good. They are supportive."

"Great. They are ready for you in the conference room." Vince left again and Riley expected the door to slam, but it shut smoothly and quietly.

"Let's not waste any time then." Craig waved his hands, and Riley ignored him. He wasn't going to let him derail his preparation.

"They will wait for me."

"You aren't a star yet."

Riley stretched his mouth into his widest grin. It seemed Craig was jealous. How interesting. "I beg to differ. This is probably one of the biggest interviews this journalist has ever had in their career. They will wait for me."

Craig's top lip curled up. "You just tell yourself that mate." He followed Vince out of the door, and Uma chuckled quietly.

"What's his problem?"

Uma rolled her eyes. "Everything. Nah, he's always been like that, but it's been worse since Stu got the promotion they both went for. Like Craig and Stu both run their own division, they are literally on the same level of the org chart as each other, but Stu got Strategy Manager and Craig got Advertising Team Leader."

"Isn't this an ad agency? Why is Strategy better?" Riley didn't really care, but he needed a moment to calm his pulse before going into this meeting.

"Strategy works closer with Vince and probably influences Vince more, I suppose. But then, Advertising runs a bigger team. I guess it depends what you think is important."

"Okay. Well, whatever. Let's go."

"True. Come on. The sooner you start, the sooner you'll be done."

Riley's heart skipped a beat. "Excuse me?"

"You look nervous, that's all. I thought that might help."

"Thanks. Sure. It helped." Riley stood up, shook out his hands, and opened the door. "Let's do this." It wouldn't be that bad would it? He'd done loads of these in his So You Think days. Surely the first few ones had been sober? Uma walked through the door he held open, and he followed her along the hallway to the conference room.

"In you go."

"What about you?"

"It's not my place. Vince will be with you as your PR manager. He said he wanted to be personally involved with this one." A little bit of awe infused Uma's voice.

"Cool."

"I mean it makes sense. You have the potential to be one of the firm's biggest clients."

Riley hadn't wanted an agent, but the contract he'd signed with Kapow had many of the same type of arrangements. They would organise all his media and interviews, and do the publicity for his music. If he decided to tour, then they had an option to assist with organising all of that too. So basically like an agency without the whole 'negotiate with record labels' bit; which Riley didn't need or want because he wasn't going down that road again.

"Go on."

"Okay. Okay. I'm going."

Uma held open the door and he stepped through. Vince leaned against the wall in the far corner of the room. Immediately as Riley walked in, Vince pushed himself away from the wall and glanced sideways. Oh, at the journalist and two camera people holding a ridiculous amount of equipment. He was in so much trouble; but not from interview nerves. All it took was one glance at Vince and the whole room disappeared. The flutter in his gut flipped and went south and he had to blink hard to focus on the actual interview.

"Hi, Riley Micah, or do you prefer Riley Le Breton? I'm Stacey Michaels. How are you?"

"Riley is fine." He shook Stacey's hand. The middle aged Chinese-American woman was one of the best music journalists in the world and they'd been lucky to get this interview with her. She was in Australia to report on a touring rock band, so naturally Riley had leaped at the chance to talk to her again. "Shall we sit?"

"Yes." Stacey nodded to her camera person. "Where do you want us with the light and stuff?"

"There is good." The camera person pointed to a couple of chairs. "Hey, Riley?"

"Yeah?"

"You look a lot younger than the photo in the paper yesterday."

Riley grinned, and for the first time today, the tension in the back of his neck eased a little. "Those photos are faked.

They literally took an old So You Think photo and ran an age filter across it."

"Seriously? That's hilarious. Did they get the calculation wrong?"

"Must have."

"You have the exclusive rights to the first images of Riley. I can get a takedown notice written up for those other ones if you wish." Vince's warm tones belied the clipped business acumen.

Elsa raised one eyebrow. "No. Leave them. We can use ours to highlight how badly they photoshopped Riley."

"That's fine with me. Before we start, I want to remind you that you've promised us an in-depth sensible interview without sensationalist clickbait headlines." Vince held Stacey's gaze and to her credit, she didn't budge. She wouldn't; she'd been doing this gig for a long time.

"Riley Micah – teen sensation rises from the dead."

A muscle in Vince's jaw twitched as Stacey joked, and Riley wanted to break the tension somehow.

"It'll be fine, Vince. Stacey interviewed me years ago when I was a teen sensation. Something I'm way too old to be anymore, even if photos showing what I'll look like when I'm seventy have been plastered all over the internet." Riley didn't need to tell Vince that he trusted her as a reporter, they'd already discussed it at length. It wasn't just the opportunity to have her by-line on a story about him, it was that she knew him from the old days and she would've done her homework.

"Seventy. More like fifty." Stacey tapped her pen on a notebook.

"I don't know what they were thinking. I've been away—"

"—but not for that long. Although a year can feel like a decade in music."

Riley relaxed at her sensible summation of what was ahead of him. Until this week, he didn't know if people would remember him, or if So You Think was a... Well, they weren't a one hit wonder, but they'd certainly faded as fast as they'd appeared.

"It has been an age since I've done anything like this."

8

Vince had a million tasks that were more important than babysitting a client through an interview, but he couldn't walk away. Any other client and he would've handed this job over to one of his many employees. Riley—Mr let's have sex once to get it out of our system—was quickly becoming embedded into his life. He wanted more than he ought to want. Being able to say 'told ya so' to himself didn't matter. He'd known he would want more than once with Riley; and he'd been right. One quick hand job against the door at his house was only the beginning. He could spend hours with his lips on Riley's skin, and fuck, licking every note on his spectacular tattoo.

"Not much has changed in the past decade. I'm going to record you on my phone." Stacey opened an app on her phone and placed it on the table in front of them.

"That's standard practice." Riley nodded and Vince reminded himself to calm the fuck down. Riley was a grown man who'd been interviewed plenty of times before. They'd discussed this during their practice runs, and they'd brainstormed all the possible nasty questions that might get asked.

"Obviously it's sensational news that you are back in the music business after a long hiatus, but I think we can warm up to the questions about what you did in the time you were away. How about we start with a short discussion about your new songs? What inspired you to write them?"

Riley eased back in his chair a little and Vince's shoulders relaxed too. "Weekend Hustler is about small town life in rural Australia. Life can be pretty harsh out there with not many opportunities, especially for young people, and the song is really about how people figure out ways to survive. I guess in some ways it's about the teenager who lives on the same street as me, who spends the week going to school and the weekends working a couple of jobs to help out the family income."

"Oh, that's super tough."

"Yes. The point of Weekend Hustler is that ambition and drive isn't something that only city people have. It's just that people in the city see more examples of people doing well. It's much harder to aspire to a better life when you can't see where you might go or how you might get there. For a kid in a small town, in straitened circumstances, to know what they need to do to improve their circumstances and the life of their family members is really special, and I wanted to speak to all those incredible people and tell them they aren't alone."

"I really like the line about a part time hustle becoming a full time victory."

"Thank you. That's the key point about the Weekend Hustler. What begins as a small way to help out family can grow into an aspiration and then into a better life for you and your loved ones."

"I love that. You've had a long hiatus between your time with So You Think and now your new releases as Riley Le Breton, do you think that time away from the music scene has changed your perspective on the world?"

Riley tilted his head and Vince held his breath. So much for giving Riley time to ease into the interview before throwing out the tough questions.

"I think time changes everyone. I mean, obviously our faces age, although not as much as a poorly photoshopped attempt that was online yesterday after my announcement…"

"Ha."

"But yes, time and I suppose what you'd call life experiences have changed my perspective on the world. From a more philosophical and I guess, literal, point of view too. Every moment, every decision we make, all impact on our future. Some choices have difficult consequences, others work out well. I mean, I don't really believe in good or bad choices. I've made many choices that people might see as bad; and perhaps in hindsight they weren't the smartest choices, but they've all led me to here. And that's not a bad thing. I don't think I could write the Riley Le Breton music with as much emotional depth without the journey I've been on."

"Wow. And as for that journey… What have you been doing since So You Think broke up?"

"Like I said yesterday during my announcement, the situation around the end of So You Think was complicated. I spent a couple of years in rehab—"

"A couple of years!" Stacey's exclamation hit Vince right in the chest. Holy fuck. Riley was no different to his father; in and out of rehab under the pretence that he wanted to get better.

"I know that sounds drastic, but for most of that time I wasn't in the intensive early part of rehab. I spent a lot of time in a wider program to ensure that I built new habits post rehab to help me stay sober. I actually ended up working at a rehab facility as a gardener doing general maintenance tasks, so perhaps my time there is blurred between being a client and being staff? Initially I thought I might be able to study and come back and help other addicts, but I realised that it wasn't healthy for me to stay there forever. I had to head out into the real world and find a way to live life, you know." As Riley talked, Vince's shoulders slowly relaxed. Riley was nothing like his deadbeat father; who hadn't tried at all. There was a self awareness to Riley's story that was starkly different to Vince's father's situation, or maybe not. Vince couldn't ignore the nagging notion that Riley was just a better actor—all addicts were actors—and he really didn't want to be involved with someone like that. Involved… What was he thinking?

"And you ended up in a small town in outback Australia?"

Riley nodded. "I wanted to go somewhere I wouldn't be recognised. I know. It sounds a bit absurd when you think about how often people messaged Triple J to say that Riley Le Breton sounded like me." Riley laughed and ran his hands through his hair. "One of my uncles knew someone who worked for the council out there, and they got me a job on a road crew. It wasn't special treatment or nepotism or anything like that. They are desperate for staff in small towns, so I just walked into the job, and since I'd been working as a gardener, I could drive the mower already and shit like that."

"But you were recognised?"

"Of course. I mean, I'd been in one of the world's biggest boy bands. I have a fairly recognisable face, I guess." Riley's smile warmed Vince all the way through. Either Riley was a brilliant actor hiding a dark secret, or he told the truth and should be admired. If only Vince knew which option was true, because his damned body kept oscillating between the two. Hot and cold.

"So the whole town was in on the secret? Your fans thought you were dead."

Riley cleared his throat and colour splashed over his cheekbones. "Firstly, I didn't know my fans thought that. I didn't look myself up online. I just wanted to be fair away from... all of that. And the town, well..." Riley breathed in deeply, and Vince realised he'd been holding his breath. "The town thought I was Paul, Riley's cousin who looked kind of like him."

"Right? And they bought that?"

Riley laughed. "You know people move to outback towns like mine for all sorts of reasons, and if I wanted to be Paul, then the locals were content to leave me be and call me Paul. I mean, after eight years, people still tease me about how much I look like Riley, so I'm pretty sure I fooled no one." He waited while Stacey chuckled. "But they all seemed to know that if I needed a place to be away from the media, then they'd let me be. I really appreciate the town for that opportunity."

"Locals stick together?"

"Yes. My first concert for Riley Le Breton will be there to thank them all for being my mates when I needed them."

Vince plucked out his phone. "Excuse me." That was the first he'd heard of it, but it was a brilliant idea. Of course, that was why Vince knew he had no chance at keeping Riley at a safe distance. The brilliant, flawed, man with an incredible body and sizzling chemistry was everything Vince didn't know he'd wanted. He had his life all planned out and was achieving his goal; to make a shit ton of money in a business he owned and controlled. If he'd earned it, no one could take it away. He might lose it through his own mistakes, but that was completely different to having it frittered away on vices. He'd learned not to need love or family. Those ideas were for other people; people who hadn't seen how it could all go wrong.

"Yes?" Stacey turned her head in his direction.

Vince glanced up from his phone. Focus. "Your article is going to press tonight, yeah?"

"Yes."

"Good. That gives us time to put some organisation stuff

around Riley's idea before it blows up." Vince sent a text to Craig to get his ad team on board with this, and to Uma who was running Riley's new social media networks. She needed to prep a few announcements to coincide with this article going live.

Elsa glanced down at her notes. "So a big launch party in a small outback town. That's a unique way to build a brand, but it does beg one question."

"Only one?" Riley's grin grew.

"For now."

"And what might your question be?"

"What town?"

"Bourke. It's about nine hours drive west of Sydney."

"Gosh, that's proper outback. I thought you might mean something between Sydney and Dubbo."

Riley shook his head. "Too close to too many people. Bourke only has about two thousand people. I mean, they have the internet and…"

"What's that grin for?"

Riley laughed. "I have a mate who gives me a Christmas card every year with Riley Micah's face on the front. Inside it says Merry Christmas Paul."

"He knew."

"Yeah. Paul is my middle name, and my mate Jordy works for the council. He's probably seen my employment contract, given that it's his job to do the hiring, but apart from the card, he pretended that I was Riley's cousin. And if he behaved like that was true, then the rest of the town shrugged and went along with it."

"So, let me get this straight. You spent two years in

rehab, some of it doing the gardening, and then you moved to Bourke where you just… what? Hung out with locals and enjoyed the spoils of So You Think?"

Riley's eyebrows flew up, and Vince realised he'd leaned forward so he straightened up to appear less keen.

"Elsa, you reported on So You Think's breakdown. You know we didn't make any money."

"That's a relative phrase. Some artists still make a decent enough income under those contracts."

"Okay, fine. My final payout was enough to fund three months full time at rehab, and when it ran out, I worked."

"As a gardener, and then in Bourke?"

"Yes. Look, it's not very glamourous or whatever might expect from the pop star life, but when the pop star thing crashes down, there's not much glitz leftover. I worked on a road crew, firstly filling potholes, then eventually I became the grader driver."

This time it was Stacey's eyebrows that rose, and the incredulous expression was probably written on his own face.

"A grader driver?" Vince mumbled the same question that Stacey asked.

Riley winked and Vince wondered what the joke was. "Come on. It's a big deal to be the grader driver. That's the unofficial foreperson of the road crew."

"Right."

"Think of it this way. If a road crew is the band, the grader driver is the lead singer, so pretty much perfect for me since…"

Elsa nodded. "You were the lead singer of So You Think."

Riley chuckled. "The crew used to tease me about being a prima donna just like my—" Riley did air quotes, "—cousin Riley. But the joke was always on them since…"

"You are Riley?"

"Nah. Because the grader drive basically runs the crew." Riley spoke without irony as he claimed the position of team leader.

"Spoken like a true prima donna." Stacey laughed and Riley ran his hands through his hair. He glanced over his shoulder at Vince and winked, and the casual gesture sent a flood of heat pulsing through Vince's veins. Damn him. Vince shuffled his feet, half ready to bolt out of the room. If he left, he could keep his head held high, having not succumbed to the impulse to march over and kiss Riley. The cockiness in his attitude was so fucking hot. He'd always found power attractive, so it wasn't much of a surprise that he was drawn to the confidence Riley demonstrated as he teased the journalist.

"And you drove this grader for how long?"

"For most of the shift. I mean it depended on what work we were doing, but out there, there are a lot of dirt roads, so we would grade them to get rid of the corrugations." Riley's smug smile was enhanced by the way his eyes danced. If he kept this up, Vince would be wrecked by desire.

"The what?"

The corner of Riley's mouth flicked up. "You don't know what a grader is, do you?"

Elsa shook her head, and Vince pulled out his phone to look it up, just to give his hands something to do. His thumb left a smudge of sweat on the screen.

"It's a big machine that has a blade underneath. You have to drive it along the dirt with the blade at the correct angle to cut the top layer of dirt off and smooth the road out so it rides well and it drains properly."

"I didn't expect the lesson in road building... fixing? And I meant how long did you work as a grader driver?"

Riley winked again. "I know what you meant. It took a while to find my feet on the crew, and then learn how to drive the grader, but I ended up on there for a few years."

"And what was the impetus for trying again with your music?" Stacey asked and Vince didn't wait for the answer. He really had better things to do than babysit Riley who had dealt with the hardest questions with aplomb. More than that, Riley had controlled where the questions went and had given answers that were cleverly filled with enough information to write the headlines and keep the newspaper happy, but without really giving away anything much. Vince hadn't expected this awareness from Riley; not when his first interview had been so terrible.

Besides, once this interview was released, the piranhas of the press were going to head to Bourke and go after Riley's friends. He needed to get his team ahead of the curve, so they knew what the next social media disaster, or revelation, might be. He slid out the door, shutting it quietly, so he didn't disturb them and paced down the hall to chat to Craig and Uma. Ella, his lawyer, should probably get involved as well, so they could better understand any other liabilities. The crunch of self-doubt in his gut grew and he pushed it away. This wasn't his first time around the block dealing with celebrity clients who needed media management. He let out a slow breath. He really didn't want to examine why this all felt different with Riley, or why he wanted to ignore all the warning signs and just kiss Riley until they both ran out of air.

"Are you alright boss?" Uma appeared in the hallway and he blinked. Had he had his head so far up his own arse that he hadn't seen her walking towards him? Hell.

"Why do you ask?"

Uma's gaze slid sideways for a second. "You sighed. And you never sigh."

"I'm good. I was looking for you." Shit. Hopefully she didn't think he sighed because she'd done something bad. It wasn't her fault, or anyone's but his own, that he was becoming obsessed with Riley. Mr once will be enough. As soon as their lips had touched, Vince had known he'd never get enough of Riley, and every moment they spent together only reinforced that. But even when he'd had lusty attractions in the past, it'd never stopped him from focusing on work. It couldn't be a clearer warning sign if it'd been tattooed on his... He swallowed. The last thing he needed right at this second was the reminder of Riley's tattoo.

"I take it you received my message about Riley's first concert." His voice came out all croaky and a frown flashed across Uma's face. He wasn't doing a bang up job of convincing her he was fine.

"Yes. I've compiled a list of potential locations and wanted to run them past Craig."

"Good. I think we have a bigger problem."

Uma's eyes widened. "Hence the sigh. I wouldn't have said the location of a concert was a problem, more like a simple piece of branding."

Vince bit back a surly response. He didn't sigh. But he'd much rather have his staff think he was worried about work than have them know he was obsessed with Riley's cock. "When this interview goes live, the world is going to know that Riley spent the last fuck knows how many years living in Bourke."

"And?"

Think. He only employed people who could think for themselves, and he'd barely finished the sarcastic thought when Uma opened her mouth.

"Oh. No wonder you are worried that the press are going to hunt down his mates, and worse, they'll find anyone in town who has a bad thing to say about him. This could blow up." Yes. She grasped the problem quickly and he let himself enjoy a fractional second of satisfaction at having employed someone capable.

"Yes. I think you and Riley should fly out there and talk to everyone first. Get a handle on whether this is going to be messy, or just you know small town and cutesy."

"Cutesy? Boss?"

Vince would not growl at her. "You know what I mean." He never lost control around his staff. Maintaining an air of aloofness was part of his personal brand, and now he was in the hallway saying shit like cutesy. Control over his body, and god forbid, his emotional state was necessary to his self of self; he required consistency, not this wild fluctuation that Riley had brought into his life.

"I do. It's quite time critical. Shall we go today?"

"Yes. As soon as they are finished the interview. Hire a helicopter or something. Get there quickly. Talk to people. You know the drill. It's the same, just way out there somewhere." Vince waved in a westerly direction. Uma nodded.

"Sure thing boss."

"One other thing."

"Yes?"

"Please call me Vince, not boss."

Uma blinked a few times. "But Craig said that you preferred it."

"He's wrong." He snapped, a fraction too loud and Uma flinched a tiny bit. Damn it. Now he was intimidating his staff in the wrong way. And fuck it, lately Craig had been more wrong than right. Part of the creative process in making ads was throwing ideas at the wall and seeing which ones the client liked, but it helped to understand the client, and recently there had been too many messes to clean up where Craig had completely misread the client and offered them something beyond the pale. That was a problem he needed to spend some time contemplating and he added it his mental tally.

"Sure thing Vince." Uma grinned and Vince let himself nod at her use of his name. "I will organise our flight now, and Riley and I can discuss potential concert locations while we are in transit."

"Perfect." And now he could get back to his office and do the thing he was good at. Making money without the pesky distraction of Riley's rich voice and hot body. He needed to figure out how to get the best from Craig—an expensive employee—in a way that would benefit Kapow's clients. Craig had been promoted to executive on the basis of some truly exceptional campaigns, but something had changed lately and Vince needed to know what it was.

9

Riley had never seen Bourke from this angle. High above, out the plane window, as they came into land. It'd been a decade since he'd been in any type of aircraft but that was in Europe where they'd been flown between gigs by the record label. It was a nine hour drive from Sydney, so he was glad Vince and Kapow Advertising splashed out for a private plane ride. The Darling River twisted its way through the town and the twin bridges marked the edge of North Bourke and the so-called border to the true Outback. It was weird seeing all his roads laid out like a map when he knew them intimately from much closer up, like that bloody corner where a car had gone off during a work site and caused endless drama when the out of towner had argued with his boss about the signs. The guy hadn't even been hurt, but he hadn't wanted to pay for the damage to his car when he'd clearly been speeding.

"Signs only work if you read them, mate."

Soon they'd land. Jordy was coming to pick them up and

the teasing was about to commence. Now Jordy would be able to gloat that he'd known all along—those bloody hilarious Christmas cards—and it was going to get rowdy. At least everyone knew Riley never went to the pub, so not that type of rowdy.

"You've sorted out the transport, Riley?" Vince asked.

"Yeah. It's no drama." Riley still didn't quite understand why Vince had come with them. Perhaps he didn't trust Uma to do her job properly, or maybe he was curious? Nah. They'd already kissed all that brilliant flash of chemistry away, so there was no reason for Vince to care about Riley outside of work. Even though this was work related—Uma and Vince wanted to meet everyone before the pests from the press tried to dig up dirt on him—yet somehow having Vince here blurred the lines between work and Riley's personal life. In reality, they'd already blurred that line by coming on each other's skin, but having Vince meet his mates was much more intimate than sex. He rolled his head on his shoulders and swallowed away the sudden moisture in his throat.

The plane landed with barely a bump, and the propellers whipped red dust around them.

"Welcome to Bourke. We'll just taxi over to the terminal building." The pilot's voice came through the earpieces. Riley closed his eyes and leaned back against the seat. He'd dozed on the way here, grateful to be sitting in the back row beside Uma who'd kept up an excited demeanour for the whole trip. Vince sat beside the pilot; just far enough away that Riley couldn't touch him. And if he kept his eyes shut, he didn't need to see the way Vince's dark brown hair curled slightly at the ends.

"You okay?" Uma asked.

"Yip."

"It's just you've had your eyes shut the whole time and I wondered if you were afraid of flying or something."

"Nope. Just snoozing."

"Okay. Cool. Is it always this dusty?"

Riley nodded. "Except when it rains, but that's not often. It rained this year for the first time in a couple of years. We got 80mm in one day, which was pretty wild." He'd been busy with his grader after that smoothing out dirt roads that hadn't coped with that much rain.

"I heard that the flowers after rain out here are pretty spectacular."

Riley grinned. "Yeah, although the smell of the gidgee tree is a bit off-putting."

"Gidgee?"

"Stinks like rotten cabbage, but only when it's wet. The old jackaroos say that it'll tell you where it's been raining." Riley would miss living out here; but then, there was no reason why he couldn't. He could write music anywhere, and there was a flight from here to Sydney a couple of days a week. And bonus, he'd be close to his mates out here.

"You can all depart now." The pilot's announcement ended with the pilot jumping out of her door and walking around to open the door on Riley's side. He jumped out and breathed in the hot, dry summer air. Ahh, summer out here smelled like red dust and a complete lack of moisture. Sweat beaded down his spine instantly as the wave of oven hot heat surrounded him.

"Fuck. I hope the hotel has air con." Vince tugged his shirt away from his body.

"Where are you staying?"

Uma glanced at her phone. "The Bourke Central Hotel."

"The pub." Riley bit back a curse. The big old pub on the centre of the main street was a local institution. He'd always avoided it because a pub where everyone socialised was the last place a sober alcoholic should go.

"Does it have aircon?"

Riley shook his head. "I have no clue. Never been inside there."

Vince frowned at him, then nodded once. "It's only for one night." Whether he referred to the heat or Riley's sobriety, Riley had no idea. He didn't want to ask for clarification.

"This way." Riley was keen to say hi to Jordy and the rest of his mates, and he'd rather not stand out here on the baking tarmac. He marched towards the small new terminal building with its green corrugated iron roof and brick façade. It looked like an old cottage with the low slung roof, a reminder of the town's colonial past. He pushed open the door and there was Jordy. He hadn't changed; well, of course he wouldn't have in the week that Riley had been away. The odd half-thought came with the realisation that he might have changed in just a week. Jordy was still the same middle aged bloke with a beer gut who hid his baldness under an Akubra. Was Riley still the quiet grader driver, or a new version of his old pop star self? Whatever. Jordy was the same as always. Friendly, open, jovial. Constant.

"Paul. Or should I call you Riley now? So good to see you. And with some fancy city folk too." Jordy winked and Riley slapped him on the shoulder.

"This is Vince. And Uma. They are my brand managers."

"Well, fuck a duck, mate. You've been gone a week and now you've got bloody brand managers."

"Hi." Vince stuck out his hand, and Jordy made a big deal of wiping on his jeans before shaking Vince's hand.

Uma squared her shoulders a little, as if she needed to brave Jordy, and held out her hand. "I'm Uma. Pleased to meet you."

Jordy shook it. "And you. Even if you are stealing my mate here."

Uma glared at Jordy and Riley shoved his mate on the shoulder.

"Jordy. Stop teasing them. You know I turned down that job because I had to give this a crack." Riley had discussed his plans with Jordy before driving to Sydney, because he was the one person in town who knew who he really was, and there was that little subject of the job Jordy had offered him. As soon as Jordy had offered him the job, Riley had known he had to take a chance on music again. He couldn't be a pen pusher at the council for the rest of his life. No disrespect to Jordy who loved the lifestyle out here; and Riley could definitely see the appeal. It was just that he had other needs; songs that wanted to be let out of his heart and set free into the world. And So You Think, for all the sins of the past, would help him do that. It was a positive way to utilise his past, better that than to let it crush him.

"Their gain is Bourke Council's loss. Come on." Jordy

spun around and walked the few steps to the door on the other side of the building.

"Um, Riley?" Uma asked.

"Yes?"

"Is there like a process or something?"

"For?"

"Arrivals."

"Nah. The pilot would've radioed ahead and done all that. They only man this place when they need." They'd left Captain Singh out with her charter plane. She would lock it up or whatever it was pilots did to their planes to keep them safe until they would all fly home tomorrow, and then presumably she'd stay somewhere in town for the evening.

Vince blinked. "And it's just unlocked the rest of the time."

"I guess so. I don't know. I mean, there's someone up in the control tower, so I guess they watch it?" Riley wasn't concerned. This was Bourke; it had issues like every other town, but it wasn't like people were going to hang out at the airport. Not when there were much better places to smoke dope and whatever. "Come on, let's jump in Jordy's car and get you guys to the pub."

Jordy chatted for the whole drive about the town, giving his guests a quick history of the place, until they pulled up outside the pub. Everyone got out of the car and Jordy grabbed their cases out of the back of his 4WD. Vince and Uma went inside, presumably to get out of the heat. Riley's pulse started to quicken at the idea of going into a pub. This was a terrible idea.

"Are you sure, Riley? Or is it cool to come in now you aren't Paul anymore?"

Riley eased out an unsteady breath. "I'd rather not, but it's where Uma booked for them, so I probably should go up and see them settled." He realised how much he'd become accustomed to his mates in Bourke picking places to socialise that didn't trigger his addiction. Uma might have read his interviews and known he'd been in rehab but without him specifically talking about what that meant on a day to day basis, she wouldn't have even given a second thought to booking accommodation in the local pub. He didn't blame her; he'd just have to chat to her about it some-time, especially if she was going to be doing all his bookings going forward.

"I can sneak you in the side door if you don't want to walk through the main bar."

"Thanks Jordy."

They walked together to the side entrance and the heat thickened, radiating off the ground and the side wall of the pub. Riley should be used to this, although he had an enclosed cab on his grader and he knew better than to go outside mid-afternoon in the summer. Only out-of-towners and a few lost souls would be outside now.

"Hey Jordy."

"Yeah, mate."

"I am sorry about the job."

"It's cool. I mean, it's not because it's bloody hard to get anyone good out here and I thought you'd make the step into the office really well."

Riley attempted to make a casual shrug. "I don't think a pen pushing job is for me."

"So if this whole music thing doesn't take off, you'll go back to the grader?"

Riley laughed. "Such faith in me."

"Just being a realist. The job, or one like it, will be there for you if you ever need it."

"Thanks, mate. I appreciate that." Riley stood on the threshold of the pub, his clammy hand on the door handle. "Look, the music is already doing well and will make me money. The problem is me. If I can stay away from the booze—" And coke and all that. "—then it'll work."

"You are tougher than you think you are. I remember when you first arrived here, a wet behind the ears townie wanting a job as a gardener."

Riley chuckled at the memory. "You said, Have you looked around here, mate? Can you see a garden? And then you offered me the job on the road crew since I could drive a mower. Thanks for taking a chance on me."

"No problem. Just don't forget us when you get all rich and fancy."

Riley swallowed. A large lump formed in the back of his throat. "I promise." He pushed open the door, holding his breath so he wouldn't breathe in the smell of the pub. His brain supplied the memory anyway, with the sharpness of gin on his tongue, but for the first time ever, all he could picture was Vince. Vince, whose kiss tasted like gin. Well, shit. Maybe he hadn't kissed it all out of his system just yet.

"Are you staying here with them?"

Riley laughed, grateful that Jordy distracted him from

84

the rising heat in his groin. "Nah. Why do that when I've got a perfectly good share house with Bryce down the road?"

"The bachelor pad."

"Something like that." Riley had rented the same cottage for eight years and his flatmates had changed a few times. Bryce worked on the road crew with him, so when his missus had walked out leaving Bryce confused and broken-hearted, Riley had invited him to stay. The two of them muddled along well enough.

"Does he know why you took a couple of weeks off work?"

Riley slowed his steps as he climbed the narrow staircase to the upper level of the pub, where all the rooms were. "He does." Riley couldn't blame the stairs on the stitch in his side. Bryce would be hurt; not just by the way Riley had lied about his identity for years, but because it came from someone he trusted. Bryce's missus had lied to him, cheated on him, and another lie from a mate was the last thing Bryce needed.

"Good. The last thing he needs is a good mate lying to him. It'll be bad enough that you pretended to be your cousin for so long." Jordy's confirmation of it was a kick to the gut. Damn it. He needed to apologise to Bryce for hiding himself for so long.

"He understands." Or rather, Riley hoped he did, because he'd explained it as best he could before he'd driven to the city. And then when the radio interview was booked, Riley had texted him with an update and Bryce had sent him a gif of someone cheering. None of that changed how fucking shitty it felt to know that he'd hurt Bryce by pretending to be someone he wasn't. For years.

"He'd better."

"Thanks for the lift, mate. I'll just see if these guys are settled in and then we can meet at the Café de Outback for dinner with everyone." Riley was caught between two worlds, but he knew one thing for certain. He didn't want Jordy to hear Vince disparage Bourke.

"If you are sure?"

"Yes. I don't need babysitting."

Hurt flashed on Jordy's face and Riley cursed under his breath.

"Sorry. I don't quite know where my head is at. Just let me chat to Vince about the plans for tonight and what they want to achieve today and tomorrow morning. I'll flick you a text or something."

Jordy nodded. "Sure, mate. Go and hang out with your new mates."

"Hey. They aren't my mates." Not yet. "And if anyone needs babysitting out here, it's them. I know I'm still finding my feet with this new job. It's literally their job to help me do that, but you know, they don't know anything about Bourke and whatever." Riley gritted his teeth. Even to himself it sounded like bullshit.

"If you say so."

Riley grinned. "I do say so." He pulled out his phone and rang Bryce. "Hey Bryce. These city slickers have set themselves up in the pub. Yeah, Jordy's here. Wanna met up in the beer garden. ... Yes, I'll be fine. You drink at our house and I'm fine. ... Yeah, I know the pub is different but it'll be outside. … Yeah. About half an hour? Cool." He hung up. "See, Bryce is going to meet you here in the beer garden. I'll go and settle these guys in, and then come down and join you. And you can both tease me about my fake identity as much as you like."

Jordy smiled, a proper grin. "I reckon there are a few others who'll want to do that too."

"Bring it on. Invite everyone who'll want to have a crack at me." Riley returned the smile and bolted up the rest of the stairs to see how Vince had settled in. Jordy's teasing about new allegiances were a little too close to the mark, and he was torn between agreeing with Jordy and being drawn to Vince.

10

Vince didn't mind a hot Sydney summer day, but damn, those days had nothing on this. The dry heat sucked the moisture out of his eyeballs and his sweat dried on his skin as fast he could produce it. He'd bolted from Jordy's 4WD—thank fuck it had aircon—into the pub and was glad the hotelier sent him upstairs to his room. A tiny room; last decorated in the 1960s if the faded green décor in the tiny ensuite bathroom was anything to go by. He'd been informed that this was their most expensive, largest room, the only one with an ensuite. Poor Uma had to use the shared bathroom, and that's why he was now in Uma's room with a single bed, a narrow window, and a sink attached to the wall. At least Uma could use a toilet without having to walk down the hallway to share a bathroom with fuck knows whoever else was staying in this actual real life Outback pub. It was much safer for her to have the room with an ensuite. He'd cope. He leaned his suitcase against the wall and turned on the fan. It swung around with a wobble and a funny noise that made him cross his fingers in case the damned thing came off the ceiling and killed him. But it was so fucking hot that Vince didn't care. He stood underneath the fan, ripped off his shirt, and let the air move over his skin. It was still too hot, even with the fan on its fastest setting. There was a knock at the door.

"Yeah, come in."

Riley stepped inside, looking way too handsome and somehow very fresh for this boiling temperature. His gaze grazed over Vince's chest and down to his groin, where his dick forgot all about the summer heat and swelled with a different sort of heat.

"Mate. How do you cope with this?" His voice cracked; totally with dehydration, not lust. He scoffed under his breath at the absurdity. Lust simmered, threatening to boil over and burn them both, more like lava flowing down a volcano than a tepid pot of water on a stove.

"You get used to it. We arrived at the worst time. It'll cool down a bit in an hour."

Vince's veins were going to explode from the combination of the fucking weather and the wide eyed way Riley stared at him. "Any other suggestions to cool down?"

Riley shrugged one shoulder, and his mouth kicked up a little on one side. "You could get naked."

"And then what?" Vince had already stripped off his shirt. He didn't think less clothes would make much of a difference.

"I don't know mate. Put your feet on ice, or something. Or maybe just ignore it. It's slightly uncomfortable but it's better than being cold."

"You could run blocks of ice all over my skin." Vince's already hard cock stiffened at the idea. Ice would melt as soon as it touched his skin, but it would stop him fainting in this ridiculous heat, and then maybe, hopefully, Riley would lick the water right off his skin. Damn.

"You'd better get nude then." Riley brushed past Vince, his shoulder barely touching, but a shiver shot up his spine. Vince didn't realise he could get any hotter. Fuck—the curse slipped out between his lips on a long needy breath. He couldn't move, just stared as Riley grabbed the single bed and pulled it away from the wall.

"What are you doing?"

"First rule of the outback in summer. Put your bed under the fan." He shifted the bed to the centre of the room and the breeze from the fan ruffled the neat edge of the dark blue pillow case.

"The fan isn't going to come loose?"

"Nah. Johnler has a good reputation around town for looking after this old place."

Vince frowned. "Johnler?"

"Yeah. Too many Johns in town, so John at the pub is Johnler. Fuck knows why. I reckon he's probably forgotten where that nickname came from. Anyway, whatever. Take off your clothes."

Vince's spine stiffened at the command. He was the one who made the rules. "Only if you take yours off too."

"Sure." Riley sat on the end of the bed, kicked off his boots, then pulled his shirt over his head. His bare torso glistened with sweat—he wasn't as unaffected by this heat as he let on—and then he unbuckled his belt and stood up. Vince scrambled to keep up. As soon as he started to take off his clothes, the relief from the sun's heat didn't arrive because the air crackled with untouched chemistry. There was only one solution; he stepped towards Riley and kissed him. Their mouths melted together, in an elemental source of strength and wonder. This was the kiss he'd been hoping for, with the taste of Riley on his lips, all cinnamon and spice with the almost overpowering overlaid saltiness from their combined summer sweat. Vince wanted more; probably more than he should want.

"You were right. Being naked is better." Vince only broke their kiss for a moment, then shoved Riley's jeans down over his hips.

Riley raked his gaze over Vince. "It is." He pushed his hands against Vince's bare chest, paced over to the beer fridge, and opened it. "Sweet. I knew Johnler would be good for it."

Way too many possibilities raced through Vince's head, and in the end only one mattered. "You can't drink."

"Relax. I'm not going to have a beer. I meant that Johnler has left ice in here."

"Ice." Vince had never wanted anything as much as he wanted the ice in the tiny fridge. Well, no, what he truly wanted was Riley to stroke his body with cubes of ice. Before he could lean towards the fridge, Riley turned around, and pushed him onto the bed. The air from the fan ruffled Riley's hair, but it was the way his body seared against him that sucked all the oxygen from his lungs. Riley bent his head and kissed him. Holy shit. Riley's mouth was full of ice and Vince had never tasted anything so incredible. Like a fucking sex ice block on a ridiculously hot day. Together they played with the ice block as they kissed, tongues and lips gliding together, as the ice melted and refreshed. A couple of drips slipped out of the corner of his mouth and left a cool trail down his cheek. Riley chased them, his lips dragging over Vince's skin as he licked the path of the ice.

"Oh, salty."

"What?" Vince's ability to form thoughts had fled in a sensory overload.

"Your skin. It's salty."

"That's good?"

Riley grinned against his cheek. "Oh yeah. It's like a hint of come and exertion and all the goodness of sex."

"Too fucking hot for sex." Vince didn't really believe it, and Riley's laugh rippled over his skin like a cool breeze. He bucked upwards against Riley's lean body, only now noticing how they matched each other perfectly. Their bodies fitted against each other in just the right way, so naturally that there was no awkwardness, no needing to figure out anything. It just worked and the simplicity made Vince's lungs expand. He reached around Riley and began to stroke his hands over his back muscles, when Riley relaxed his mouth and dropped a lump of ice onto Vince's throat. The swift shock almost had him yelping, but Riley shifted off him and began to trace the quickly melting ice over his chest. His nipples were hard points, and he wanted to purr as the ice gave him relief from this heat. The slight breeze from the overworked fan met with the trail of cool water and it was all he could do to stop himself groaning and begging for more.

"Give me a second." Riley leaped off the bed and Vince half sat up. The water had already started to evaporate by the time Riley came back with a handful of ice. He spread it over Vince's stomach, letting some drip into his belly button, and took his time to trace the ice all over his chest, shoulders, arms, everywhere. Just as Vince thought he might drown in the careful way Riley used the ice to cool off his overheated body, Riley leaned over him, sucked the last remaining piece of ice into his mouth and then licked the end of Vince's cock. Oh fuck me now.

"Alright."

Had he said that out loud? He didn't regret begging for Riley's dick, he was desperate for his touch, even though it made zero sense to want sex while the air sweltered and that bloody fan made a constant knocking sound, just out of time with his pulse. Ha—his heart rate zoomed at least twice as fast as the damned fan.

"I don't think ice would make great lube, and I don't have any condoms." Riley's eyebrows smashed together in a thoughtful frown.

"I don't have any either, but never mind that, we can still—"

"—There are plenty of other ways I can make you scream with pleasure."

"Mate. I don't scream." Vince might grunt or groan, but scream. Nah.

Riley's frown disappeared, replaced with a cheeky grin. "Wanna bet?"

"Sure." Vince wanted to know what Riley would do

next; he had a creative musical mind, which meant anything was possible.

"Do you have anything you don't like?"

Aside from not being in control… "This fucking heat."

"Not much I can do about that." Riley jumped up again, and the sight of his lean body effortlessly moving off the bed was surely the reason Vince lurched backwards. Every muscle shifted under his skin like he was designed for artistic photography—no wonder he'd been selected as the lead for a boy band when he was a teen. In the decade since, Riley's body must have changed, but he was still lean and pretty, with a hardness about him in the way he held himself. He leaned over and opened the little beer fridge again; gifting Vince with the perfect sight of his arse. Vince swallowed. As soon as the glimpse was there, it was gone again, replaced, as Riley spun to face him. Riley's hard cock and that fucking tattoo of his; all musical script on clean shaven skin was the best view in the universe. Last time, his pubes had been clipped short so the tattoo peeked out, but now Riley had shaven himself so the tattoo replaced the usual black hairs. Now that was artistry; the dark ink around Riley's large beautiful cock was instagrammable, and yet Vince wanted to keep it all for himself. He was selfish enough not to share something so picturesque with the world. His. Vince shivered at the sudden intense notion. Riley thought this would fade, and Vince may as well remind himself to get accustomed to that idea before he fell any harder for Riley.

"We are almost out of ice."

"What a tragedy. Come here." Vince sat up. It was time

to take charge of this situation—just as he preferred—and he held out his hand. "Give that to me."

Riley's gaze darted sideways. "That being the ice or my dick?"

"Both." Vince licked his impossibly dry lips. This damned heat; it was so dry, his sweat didn't even have time to drip. It just evaporated. His dry mouth had nothing at all to do with the sight of Riley standing at the end of the bed, fully erect and lovely, holding out a handful of dripping ice. Nothing. Everything. He shifted to the end of the bed and wrapped his fist around Riley's hand. The ice water seeped out, over his skin, and he gasped.

"Hell, Vince. This bet is all mine."

"What?"

"If you gasp from a little touch of our hands, it'll be easy to make you scream."

"It's the bloody ice."

Riley raised one eyebrow. "Sure it is."

"Right. That does it." Vince grinned, then pushed Riley's hand against his chest. This time it was Riley who gasped as icy cold water splashed over his chest and started to drip down his abdomen. Vince leaned forward and licked the water, slowly making his way upwards until he found Riley's nipple ring and he tugged with his teeth. The sharp intake of breath and the way Riley's chest rose and fell quickly was worth it, but Riley surprised him as usual. He dropped his hand and grabbed Vince's throbbing cock. The cool flesh of Riley's hand, almost frozen from holding the now-melted ice, against the needy heat of his dick was almost too much. He hissed.

"Almost."

Vince tugged Riley's nipple ring again, but his mouth ended up sliding up towards Riley's shoulder and it took far too long to realise that Riley was slowly lowering himself until he kneeled on the floor in front of Vince. Vince threaded his hands through Riley's hair and was rewarded when Riley's tongue flicked over the end of his cock. He barely had time to register the flash of desire before Riley opened his mouth and sucked him inside. The warm heat of Riley's mouth was so different to the desiccating dry air. It was a bloody oasis, or some shit like that. His brain stopped working and it was all he could do to lean back on his hands and focus on the way Riley's floppy black hair looked as he sucked him deep into his mouth. Vince held on tight to the blanket, needing an anchor as Riley's tongue and mouth sought out every inch of pleasure. His balls tightened and he gasped. He would not come in Riley's mouth. That seemed important even if he couldn't remember why; couldn't make his thoughts coherent because his whole world was focused on the way Riley's flattened tongue allowed his dick to sink all the way into his throat.

"Holy fuck." He whispered, a hoarse desperate noise, and he clung tighter to the bed. But Riley didn't let up, he only increased the speed with his lips tight around Vince's shaft, and then he cupped Vince's taut balls and slid his thumb across his arse. Vince grasped Riley's hair and pulled as release beckoned. Riley sank down once more, deeper than ever before, then dragged his mouth up the length of Vince's cock with just a hint of teeth against his sensitive skin. Dangerous and fucking perfect. Vince let out a strangled cry as Riley's mouth popped off the end of his cock, and Vince came in a guttural rush. Come spurted all over his skin, on Riley's throat and hand, and Vince didn't care because his release was so hard, so sudden, and so intense, little white spots appeared in his vision. Riley milked his cock with a relaxed grip and Vince flopped back on the bed.

"Told you."

"What?" Vince croaked.

"I'd make you scream."

Vince cracked one eye open and got a face full of Riley's smug smile. "Yeah. What do you win?"

"You probably should've established that beforehand. Too fucking … cocky … for your own good."

"Hell, Riley." If it were anyone else, Vince would've hated this sense of coming undone for someone. Come to think of it, he'd never had this before; never been utterly wrecked by someone's mouth to the point where he'd come without caring for his partner. He cleared the sudden lump in the back of his throat. "Um, Riley?"

"Yeah."

"Do you need…"

"Nah mate. I'm all good. I came when you did."

"You did?" Shit, Vince was even more gone than he'd realised. So caught up in the delicious way Riley's mouth covered him that he hadn't noticed Riley's own pleasure.

"What is that look?"

"What look?" But Vince knew. It was guilt at his own selfishness, either that or panic because he never allowed himself to become lost in the moment. And what did that loss of control mean? Nothing. It was a temporary issue caused by… Vince sucked in a short breath, the hot air burning across his tongue and into his lungs.

"Nothing. It doesn't matter."

A breath of cool air brushed over his skin and Vince realised it was relief that Riley hadn't pushed him to explain. "Let's get cleaned up." Vince scrambled backwards on the bed, then swung his legs off the side, and glanced around the tiny room for a towel or something. Anything he could use to wash his stomach. His knees wobbled a bit as he stood up —just a little bit of pins and needles from the way he'd been sitting—yeah, right. He needed to stop trying to kid himself over the way he was drawn to Riley.

A loud bang on the door clanged through the room and he jumped. "Yeah?"

"I hope it's locked." Riley's whisper had a hint of laughter in it. There was an unfairness to the way Riley didn't sound at all wrecked by this, while Vince—who normally kept a controlled distance with sex—could barely function. Air rushed in and out of his lungs as he scrambled to regain his balance.

"So do I."

"It's Uma. Um, I have a small problem."

"What?"

"Can I come in?" She sounded like she was pressed right up against the keyhole.

"Not really. What's the matter?" Vince grabbed a towel, ran it under the tap and washed himself. He did the same with the other end of the towel and held it out for Riley.

"It's confidential."

"Just spit it out, Uma." Vince didn't want to deal with

work problems. He should be cleaning Riley and kissing him. Thank you. That's what he should be doing; like a gentleman or some shit because then he might... No, he had a snowballs chance in hell of squaring off this and asserting some authority over the situation. Riley obviously just wanted a fuck or two and then to carry on with his plans to write best-selling music, and if Vince wasn't careful, he'd be left behind, like the dirty water churned up by a boat engine.

"No one can find Riley." Her whisper squeaked and Riley laughed quietly. The sound washed over Vince's body and he shivered.

"I'm in here with Vince."

"Yeah, we are just going over the plan for tonight."

Riley winked, then held his now softening cock. "More of this." He stroked himself and Vince closed his eyes for way too long.

"Oh, okay then." Uma's voice rose in volume. "Well, everyone else is downstairs in the beer garden. I'll just tell them that we've found him, and it's all good. Will you meet me down there?"

"Yes." Vince stopped himself from saying anything else. He was the boss. It was no one's business if he chose to spend his time like this. Except for the whole part where it was his idea to come to Riley's town and interview all his mates to ensure they weren't going to get surprised by anything else.

Riley's surprise revelation that he'd gone to rehab had been enough of a shock. Vince couldn't take another one. A chill spread across his back and chest. What the fuck was he doing with Riley? An addict. It was everything he had promised himself he would never become involved with again. He couldn't go through the wild ups and downs of his childhood again. He grabbed his clothes and shoved them on, almost brutally. He needed to get out of here, into the air where he could breathe properly. Away from the stifling lack of oxygen in this room; and it wasn't the summer heat he referred to.

"Come on then. Let's meet your mates." He threw on a clean shirt from his suitcase, grabbed the key for his crappy little country pub room, and bolted out of the room, leaving Riley to sort himself out. So what if it made him a shitty lover. He literally couldn't breathe in there anymore.

11

Riley had barely time to smile at the way Vince looked in his post-sex haze when Uma's interruption wiped the dazed expression away. He didn't know what she said or why, but Vince's voice changed from sexy and husky to a rude growl. Vince had fled; there was no other way to describe the way he'd grabbed the key and bolted out of the room. As Riley put his clothes back on, he ran back over the conversation with Uma, but there were no clues. Vince hadn't seemed bothered when they might have been caught together—neither was he—because they were adults and honestly it was no one's business. He hadn't exactly been honest, but he didn't give off a secretive vibe during that part of the conversation. He'd grinned at Riley as if they had a delicious secret, one that Vince wanted to hold close and keep and it'd filled Riley with a rich warmth like pumpkin soup on a cold day. It wasn't until Uma had left that Vince seemed to figure out something; but he left no clues for what had triggered the change or what that worry might be. Riley tucked that mystery away for another time. First things first, he needed to get roasted by all his mates. He turned the fan down to a less dramatic level and it lost that out of kilter rattle. He stepped into the hallway, closed the door to Vince's room, checked that it was locked with a shake of the doorknob, and made his way down to the beer garden.

"Paul. Paul. Over here." Bryce stood up with a massive grin on his face.

"Or is it Riley now?" Chris, one of the other guys on the road crew, laughed and stood up with his hand outstretched for a solid handshake.

Suzy shoved Chris on the shoulder, then shook Riley's hand as well. "Maybe we should call him Paulmy; like your bro Johnler's nickname."

"Johnler isn't my bro." Chris's grin broadened.

"Nah, he's your…"

"Partner. Suzy, you can call him my partner."

Suzy flung her head backwards and cackled. "Awesome, man. I thought it was just a one night stand or something."

Chris blushed a little, his skin darkening across his cheeks. "Or something. We figured that we had to call it something else. A one night stand doesn't really last for six months!"

"Good for you two." Riley had slept with Chris years ago when he'd first move here, but they hadn't really had much chemistry so nothing more had come of it. He was thrilled his two mates, Chris and Johnler, had finally seen sense and hooked up properly. He'd never been tempted to have a one night stand with Johnler—he smelled like his job—actually, that wasn't quite true, on either count. He'd never gotten close enough to Johnler to smell him, but he worked with Riley's nemesis—alcohol—so he was kind of off limits. In some ways it was a shame. There weren't that many openly gay men out here, so it had crossed his mind that Johnler could be an option if he'd ever wanted more than his hand or one of the few widowed farmers wives who came into town for supplies on occasion.

God, that made him sound like a dick, but he had had a couple of quiet arrangements with some lovely women over the years and he appreciated their discretion and vis versa. Lucy at the pharmacy had flirted with him for years; he was pretty sure she'd figured out that the whole *Paul my cousin is Riley Micah* thing was a lie. And he hadn't been ready to open up that part of his life just yet. His sex life in Bourke happened at a lot slower pace than when he'd been a teen idol, but he didn't mind the change of pace. Better to have a few partners over the years and remember everything than the mindless whoring of his youth.

"You alright, Paul? I mean Riley."

"Yeah, sure."

"You just zoned right out there for a while." Chris leaned in closer and whispered. "Johnler knows about us from ages ago and he's cool with it."

"I'm cool with it too. I'm really glad you are happy." Riley paused for a second. "You are happy?"

Chris's wide grin told him everything. "I am."

"What about you Paul? Riley. You've been gone from town for a week and now you are famous again, but are you happy?" Suzy quizzed him and he tried his best not to glance at Vince.

"I—" He nearly lied and said he was, but a little burr in the back of his throat stopped him. "I am cautiously optimistic. Bryce will tell you that I've been planning this for ages; he's had to listen to all my songs as I learned them and recorded them."

"Hey Bryce." Suzy called out to their other mate and Riley turned his head to see Bryce standing awkwardly on one leg chatting to Uma. "You were in on this? Mate." She drew out the last word and Riley shooshed her.

"I didn't exactly tell him everything. He just heard me playing my guitar and stuff, and he knew I was going to Sydney for something to do with my music, but I didn't tell him the whole story."

"And why not? We are your mates." Chris and Suzy spoke in unison.

"Yeah. I'm sorry."

"Didn't you trust us?" Suzy asked.

"Nah, I trust you. It's just that, well—" Riley glanced around the beer garden, at the mostly empty tables with faded sun umbrellas over them, and the two big gum trees at the back near the carpark. This life was so different to So You Think. He drew a deep breath in through his nose, the perfume of the dry air filling his nostrils, and he realised the issue.

"What?"

"I really like you guys. You are my mates and I guess I didn't want you to change around me." Too many people became sycophantic when they knew he was famous. He'd been there and he hadn't been able to tell who was a true friend and who was just pretending for selfish reasons.

"Who said anything about changing? You'll always be Paul to us." Suzy paused. "What should I call you? I can't stop thinking of you as Paul, but…"

"Paul is my middle name. I'm okay with either." He'd been Riley for longer, but like Suzy said, he was used to being called Paul when he was here. He'd been Paul for nearly a third of his life now. Weird. Vince tapped him on the shoulder and he nearly leaped out of his skin at the pulse of electricity.

"Hi. Does anyone want a drink before we do introductions?" Vince asked, and Riley tensed. He shouldn't have agreed to being here, even though he'd coped with Bryce having a beer on a Friday night after work every week at home.

"Pub squash for me." He ground it out between his clenched teeth. The others gave Vince their orders and he disappeared back into the pub.

"Mate, I forgot you don't drink. Is it weird to be here?" Chris asked.

In the interests of honesty, Riley nodded once. "A little, but it's fine. Look, just a heads up, Vince is going to be my PR manager for my music and he wants to know all the gossip about me."

"And you are alright with that? Sounds a bit city." Suzy sneered a little and Riley nearly choked holding back a laugh.

"So basically you guys don't give a shit that I was famous once?"

Chris shook his head. "Speak for yourself man. I think it's pretty fucking cool."

"Plus, I reckon you are pretty famous right now. I've listened to those songs of yours on the radio. It's quite weird to know that it's you. I didn't even know you could sing."

Bryce shoved Suzy on the shoulder. "He bloody sings every day in the shower. Makes a fucking racket!" And with that one comment, Riley knew the world was still fine. These people would always be his mates, no matter where his music took him in the world, he'd always be welcome here. A prickle itched at the corner of his left eye, but he was saved from his own sappiness when Vince and Johnler arrived carrying a tray of drinks.

"Congratulations, Johnler."

"For?" The whippet thin tall publican tilted his head and the sunlight caught his earring with a glint.

"Chris told us you two were an item." Suzy chuckled, "But I already knew that."

"Yeah, you gossiping old biddy, always holding up one end of the bar."

"What are you talking about? You know more about everyone in town than they know about themselves, I reckon."

Johnler winked. "Just doing my job. Part publican, part therapist." He slid the tray of drinks onto the table, then half bowed and Suzy roared with laughter.

"Hey everyone. Sorry I'm late." Jordy joined them. He was wearing his best shirt and his good hat. "It takes a while to get this face all prettied up."

Rowdy laughter rang around the garden, and Riley's

shoulders relaxed. He expected his friends to harass him and make fun of his situation, but they just carried on as usual and it was really lovely. Exactly what he needed to ground himself. He tapped his glass of pub squash.

"Um, everyone. I'm just going to do a couple of introductions. As you know, I'm not really Paul. I'm Riley Paul Micah, also known as Riley Le Breton." No one made a sound, so he carried on. "It sounds a bit pathetic, but I only meant to stay in town for a short while, a year at most, so it didn't matter if no one knew I wasn't really Paul. One year turned into eight, and I guess it just became habit. So I'm sorry about that." Riley realised he'd been staring at his boots, so he forced his head up and made eye contact with his friends.

"Thanks mate. I appreciate the honesty." Bryce's voice rang out in a clear whisper and everyone nodded. Right, he needed to do something else before he bloody cried or something.

"Anyway, a couple of introductions. This is Vince who is managing my PR and all that stuff. And this is Uma. She—"

Vince interrupted. "—She does all the actual work." Vince's joke broke the odd silent tension and Suzy clapped.

"Go Uma. Someone has to show the blokes how to get things done."

"Yeah, and Vince and Uma, these are my best mates." Riley waved his hand at each of them as he introduced them. "Suzy. Chris, Johnler who runs the pub, Jordy. Um, and my flatmate, Bryce." Riley sipped his pub squash, thankful for that Johnler had made it with seventy percent ice to reduce the amount of sugar in the lemon flavoured soft drink.

Jordy cleared his throat. "Hey, you know what's funny, Paul. Riley."

"What?"

"Mate, you are your own cousin and so is Bryce."

Bryce rolled his eyes. "For the last bloody time, I'm my own step-cousin. Step."

"How does that work?" Uma asked. Riley laughed at her wide eyed expression as Bryce flung his head back and barked out a raucous laugh.

"Small towns. That's how it works."

"But?"

"So your cousin is someone who has the same grand-parent as you, right. Like the kid of your aunt or uncle."

"Yes, but how do you get to be your own cousin?"

"My mum's second husband is my aunt on dad's side's first husband. So I'm my own step-cousin." Bryce laid it out as if it were obvious. From the way the two city dwellers were staring at him, they probably didn't think it was obvious. It must be a small town thing.

"Come on." Riley laughed. "I'm my own cousin because I was pretending to be Riley's cousin but I'm just me. Bryce is his own cousin because his dad's sister was married but then they broke up, leaving his uncle free to go off and marry his mum."

"Step-cousin. And mate, it's not the same at all. You lied to us and told us you were Paul who just happens to look like his famous cousin Riley."

"Like I said, Paul is my middle name."

"Still a lie." Perhaps Bryce's early forgiveness wasn't as black and white as Riley had assumed. It made sense since Bryce had trust issues for good bloody reason, but Riley had hoped that wouldn't affect their friendship. Well, he'd just keep working at it and proving himself.

Uma cleared her throat. "So, Bryce, a question?"

"Yeah?"

"Wouldn't that make family dinners a bit awkward?"

Bryce shrugged. "Nah. Aunt Sarah never had kids with Fred, and they just kind of drifted apart. It was years before Fred hooked up with Mum."

"Okay." The way Uma looked at Bryce reminded Riley of the way he stared at Vince and his chest swelled a little. The connection he had with Vince should scare him, but it didn't. Not when it gave him this moment. If Bryce found happiness with Uma, even if it was temporary, that would be amazing. Standing here in the beer garden while his friends laughed and talked shit was so grounding. He needed to find a way to be ambitious with his music but also keep his mates around him.

Now that he'd left—just for a week—he'd almost forgotten how stifling this town had become. Not the heat, but the way he was pretending to be a smaller version of himself until he couldn't live without music anymore. Part of the lie he'd lived here was to never play his guitar around his friends, well, except Bryce who lived in his house. Until a week ago, Riley treated playing guitar around the house was just a hobby, that was all. His good guitars were still in storage in his parent's garage. He visited his parents twice a year, spent time with them, and listened to his father's quiet well-meaning lecture on how he should have done accountancy not music because then he'd have a more stable income. There was love there, he'd had a good childhood, but his parents had never understood his drive to be a musician. In their eyes, it was a hobby, not a job, hence why it was easy to pretend to Bryce that he only played for a bit of fun.

A couple of years ago, he'd been ready to play the much neglected instruments again. It'd taken a long time to come to terms with the idea that his parents might be right. He'd tried to be a musician and the lifestyle had been too much for him. Slowly, as he healed, the yearning in his soul for music grew again until he'd spent a few days in his parent's garage doing all the maintenance on his neglected instruments. He'd cleaned them all, and restrung them, then had taken the cheapest one back to Bourke. The sharp contrast between this week in Sydney and being here again reminded him of the good parts of Bourke—friendship, being welcomed, having people who cared about him. He knew exactly how much the music industry cared for him. Zilch. He needed to balance both the need to be fully himself with his music while staying sober and retain these friendships and their importance to him. A Herculean task but if anyone could pull it off, it was him. He chuckled quietly—spoken like a true lead singer.

12

———

Vince couldn't wait to get Riley home to his apartment. He needed more; more than a quick fuck in a sticky hotel room with no aircon. Riley's friends were great, and it was obvious they didn't need to worry about them telling the nastier elements of the press awful things about Riley. Not just because there didn't seem to be any awful things about Riley, but also because they rallied around him and protected him from outsiders. Riley had come here to stay clean and seemed to have achieved it. A flicker of a memory told him not to trust that; addicts were liars; but he pushed it away. Riley wasn't Vince's deadbeat dad.

He spent the rest of the evening watching and listening for potential troubles, but everyone was really kind to each other in a rowdy country kind of way, and he slowly relaxed. At some point Jordy pulled him aside and they talked about Riley's future. Even with Vince fishing for details, he didn't find any potential issues for the press to highlight. Riley had kept his head low in town, had been a great employee, and even volunteered at the church's soup kitchen. A good citizen.

"He was a bit like an unbroken brumby when he first came here. Nervous and jumpy, but he settled in over time." Jordy sipped his beer. "He keeps to himself mostly; doesn't go to the pub, doesn't play sport. It's funny how he's made friends because he's a bit of a city boy. I guess it's not really a surprise to know he was hiding something."

"But he said you knew his real name."

"Yeah. I knew he was using his middle name, but plenty of people have reasons to hide. Maybe he was running from a bad relationship or something. Not really my business you know."

"And I guess boy bands aren't really your thing?" Vince teased.

Riley clapped Jordy on the shoulder. "If it's not eighties rock, or proper country music, then it's not real music, is it Jordy?"

"Very true. I don't understand the appeal of all that doof doof stuff."

"Can you see why I could just be me out here? No one listens to So You Think." An edge to Riley's voice made Vince wonder if that was the whole truth. Was Riley really himself when people didn't know about his biggest success? Vince swallowed down a sarcastic snort—he was probably projecting his own drive for success onto Riley's life—reading too much into an awkward social moment.

"I reckon some of the school kids did, but most of them leave town so you were safe from the teens who would've remembered. They were all gone by the time you got here."

Riley laughed, and the sound rippled over Vince's sticky skin. The worst of the heat had died down, just as Riley had predicted, but it was still bloody hot. "I reckon Lucy at the pharmacy knew. She had a poster of So You Think up behind her desk when I first came to town. Had to keep my hat tugged down low whenever I went in there or walked past. Lucky I'm healthy as an ox, so I only went in there every couple of years."

"What do you guys do for entertainment in the evenings here?" Vince switched the subject away from Riley's healthy body. He'd had his hands all over him and he knew exactly how fit and lean Riley was, and he wanted more. He lifted his chin a touch, he was proud of the control he had over his body. He really didn't want to contemplate why all that legendary control disappeared—evaporated like his sweat in this heat—whenever Riley was near. Even standing here beside him had him practically vibrating with lust, and worse, with curiosity to know everything there was to know about Riley. Nah, that was just work, nothing more. *Yeah, keep telling yourself that, Vince.*

"This." Jordy stared at him as if he'd sprouted two heads. "What do city types do?"

Vince chuckled. He'd much rather talk about something innocuous than dwell on the way Riley messed with his carefully curated steadiness. "I usually work late at the office, eat dinner at my desk, and then keep working until I have to sleep before doing it all over again." It sounded like a crap life when he laid it all out like that, and he nearly made a joke about work hard, play hard but held it back for Riley's sake. Besides, he loved his work and putting in the hours was what he needed to do to hit his goals. He had to build up what had been taken away from him. The sharp reminder of his life plan was exactly what he needed to shut up the internal chatter about Riley.

"Mate, you need to move out here for the lifestyle. Work for the council, you'll finish by mid-afternoon, then you can go fishing on the river, or go camping, or other fun shit." Jordy grinned. "I've been doing up an old truck in my shed."

"I don't think that life is for me." Vince let the disdain he felt colour his tone. He hadn't become this rich by being polite.

"You can't take the money with you, mate."

Riley glanced between them both. "It's okay to have different goals in life."

"Is this how you have so many mates that defend you even after you lied to them about who you are? You are a peace keeper; someone who keeps the party going because you stop arguments." Vince's attempt at humour fell flat as everyone stared at him like he'd sprouted broccoli from his teeth.

"Tell me what you really think." Riley's voice hardened.

"Did I say something wrong?"

"Nah." Riley shrugged and walked away to talk to someone else. Vince stared after him.

"It's an interesting choice to treat a client like that." Jordy frowned, his face reflecting the twists inside Vince's stomach. Client; yeah, that's what everyone here thought of their relationship. He probably looked like a creep staring at the way Riley's tight arse moved as he walked with a rigid spine away from him. He sucked in a deep breath.

"It's symbiotic. You wouldn't understand."

"Because I'm just a country council worker? Careful, city boy." Jordy walked away, leaving Vince with no choice but to head up to his room and retire for the night. He wasn't running from a fight—not at all—he just had emails to get through and this thing with Riley had probably gone as far as it could. He'd check in with Craig for an update. This morning's interview should be live now and there should be an impact on Riley's song sales and downloads online. He also wanted to talk to Craig about how he was dealing with this new business. Craig's team had put together all the graphics and advertising for Riley; creating his website with all the right links and look. Uma was one of the social media experts who ran all of Riley's accounts for him, and she currently sat in Craig's team. It seemed to be working, but a CEO's job was never done and maybe he should talk to Stu about strategy and how to build on this opportunity to do PR for more clients. A baby idea began to form as he bounded up the stairs towards his room.

Vince's alarm rang as usual at six the next morning and he shut it down with an angry stab of his finger. He'd already been awake for hours, unable to sleep in this persistent heat with the fucking fan threatening to come loose and murder him in his bed. His phone pinged with a message.

Riley: You awake?

Vince: Can't fucking sleep in this heat.

Riley: Come for a swim with me.

Hell yes. He shut his eyes for a second, indulging in the idea of cool water surrounding his body. He leaped out of bed to run to Riley. No, to the pool. Fuck. He paced in a circle, mimicking the bloody fan. How the fuck did one person get him so off kilter? He was Vince Cattaneo. Owner of the biggest advertising agency in the southern hemisphere. Grandson of one of Australia's first billionaires. He was the boss. Not someone who chased after someone with his tongue hanging out. He'd sworn to himself that he would be the one people chased after. Never again would he be the one who chased someone, desperate for the tiniest hint of love. Sweat dripped down his spine. This argument with himself was pointless. He wanted a swim and if Riley happened to be the one who suggested it, he shouldn't spite his own body just because he was having complicated feelings. Feelings. Fuck that.

Vince: Where?

This would be a lot easier if Riley was only a client with a smoking hot body and sex was purely about chemistry and lust. The real problem was that he liked Riley.

Riley: Public pool. Nowhere else to swim in summer. River is too low.

Vince: 10 mins

He was sure he could get there in ten minutes, wherever the pool was. This town wasn't that big. He opened the map app on his phone and searched for the pools. Yeah, see, only a five minute walk from his room. He flung on some undies that would do for a swimming costume—they were so close to Queensland here—did they call them swimmers or cossies? Shut up brain. Clearly he hadn't slept enough. He needed a coffee or three.

Clothes, shoes, a towel, his phone, the room key. Yip, he was ready. He marched to the pool, sweat making his shirt stick to his torso. Even this early in the day it was still warm enough that any exertion made him sweat. He arrived at the two prefabricated buildings in the middle of a grassy park and handed over his gold coin for entry. Some things in the country were pretty cool. It was a heck of a lot cheaper to go for a swim. He strode into the fenced pool area to see a toddler pool under a huge canopy, with a 50m Olympic sized pool behind. A few swimmers took up a couple of lanes, gliding through the water. Vince sat down on a hard bench and stared off into the distance. The water looked incredibly inviting, yet it seemed rude to jump in without Riley. He ran his hand through his hair. This whole situation had him more messed up than he'd ever been in his life. He didn't do confused. And he certainly didn't do relationships or anything that might resemble love or family or whatever. It should be simple—fuck him then fuck off—just like he preferred. A gentle touch on his shoulder made him jump in his seat and he twisted around to stare at Riley.

"Hey. You okay?"

Vince cleared his throat. "Slept like crap in the heat, but yeah, I'm okay."

"Let's go." Riley sauntered past him and Vince jumped up off the wooden bench. He paced past him and couldn't resist slapping Riley on the arse as he went past. It served him right for wriggling it at him as he waltzed away, deliberately tempting. Vince cursed the way he succumbed to Riley's wiles and threw himself into a run, then dove into the pool. Oh my god—cool water slipped over his skin like heaven. He surfaced with a grin only to get a face full of water.

"Hey!"

Riley laughed and slapped the surface again, sending another spray of water towards him. Vince dove under the water and grabbed Riley by the legs. If they were going to play like silly teenagers, then he'd better get all the advantages he could. Before he could run his hands up Riley's strong thighs, Riley kicked out and spun away. Vince couldn't take his gaze off him, the way the water flowed over his muscles, the bulge of his hip flexors only barely covered by his shorts, and the strength in his legs and arms. Every muscle was honed, and Vince thanked the cool water for being the only reason he wasn't sporting the world's hardest erection. A minute with Riley made all his cogitating pointless. He couldn't resist Riley and from the second Riley had touched him he'd forgotten why he had declared that he should. It was a lot of bother to hold himself away, and for what? It wasn't like he had any moral principles about sex, especially not when it was this good.

Riley called over his shoulder. "Race you?" Then took off, leaving Vince in his wake. Vince breathed in deep, then stretched out in the pool, racing after him. He'd been a reasonable swimmer at high school but hadn't ended up in the squad team for reasons. Complicated reasons that he'd do well to remember. As he closed in on Riley's splashing feet, Vince cursed his upbringing for making this moment much more complex than it ought to be. He should be happy, just enjoying being in cool water on a stinking hot morning under the bright Aussie sun, with his lover in front of him.

"Beat you." Riley rested against the end of the pool, his usually floppy black hair all slick against his temples.

Vince stood in the laneway, perhaps ten metres from Riley, having stopped mid-stroke. "Yeah, you did." His lungs cried out for air. He really needed to get back to Sydney and remember what the fuck he was doing with his life. This was a lovely interlude to life, but it couldn't be anything more. Not with an addict. What was he thinking?

"You left early last night."

"I had work to do." It wasn't exactly the whole truth.

Riley raised one eyebrow. Yeah, Vince didn't believe himself either. "You didn't miss much. Uma came home with us."

"What my employees do on their own time is not my business." Vince shrugged. Provided she turned up to work with all her energy and focus, then the rest of her choices were irrelevant to him.

"Yeah. Well, they talked and I wrote a new song."

"In other words, you were working late too." He deliberately made the statement smug and even raised one eyebrow to complete his point.

"It's called The life of the party."

Vince almost laughed but he still had no air in his lungs. It was like the summer breeze stole it all from the back of his throat and he struggled to figure out where all the oxygen had gone. He wasn't unfit; less than one length of the pool shouldn't make him pant like this. Then he remembered he'd said exactly that last night before Riley bolted away. Funny how his body knew before his brain kicked in, but then most of his blood had gone south as he stared at Riley. The man—his lover—stood with one elbow on the edge of the pool with little rivulets of water dripping off his hair. He should be on the front cover of a magazine looking like that, or on posters bought by fans to hang in their bedrooms.

"Okay?"

"Want to hear it?" Riley's gaze dropped to Vince's mouth for a second, so quickly that Vince would've missed it if he wasn't so utterly focused on him.

"Now?" He'd much rather kiss Riley than watch him sing.

"No. I'm not going to sing my new song here in the pool, like some sort of weirdo. There could be cameras recording us."

Vince's mouth dried. "Is that why you are leaning there like that?" Posed and picture perfect.

Riley flicked his hair off his face. "Sure." But then he ran his gaze over Vince and Vince took a half-step backwards. On anyone else, Vince would read that as an invitation, a blatant one. He hadn't spent years as a rich businessman without many, many people issuing such obvious invitations. It couldn't be this time, though because Riley had literally just talked about being on camera. He wouldn't, not with the possibility of the press watching. Vince must have misread it.

Riley invited Vince to the pool because he wanted a swim and they needed to talk. Last night, he'd been angry with him and instead of arguing over the details, like they should over a misunderstanding, Vince had slunk off to his room before Riley had the chance to confront him. Riley had gone home to the house he shared with Bryce and poured all that energy into a new song. Now that was done, he needed a swim to relax, just like he used to do after work when he lived here. Scratch that, he still lived here. And he'd asked Vince to drop by the pool because they still needed to have the argument about it. Plus, he was proud of the new song and he wanted to share it with someone. The bassline drummed in his head—it didn't even exist yet outside his brain—only the lyrics and the melody that he'd plucked out on his guitar and recorded into his phone. Once he added some layers, this song would vibrate through people's chests and make them want to jump. He had been the life of the party once and it'd damn near killed him. Never again. Never again. He wanted both the energy of being the lead singer and none of the downside at the same time. Was it possible?

The throbbing in his veins built up as he'd walked to the pool, but all that energy dissipated in a rush as Vince smiled and played in the water. His broad shoulders and gym-sculpted body moved with ease in the quiet water of the public pool. Riley's heart still thumped and his blood still raced through his veins, but it was to a different beat. An urgent needy beat. He'd mentioned cameras because other-wise he was going to jump Vince in the pool and kiss him until they drowned in each other's desire. In public, where anyone might see. He dunked his hands in the cool water, then splashed it up over his hot face.

"Have you done everything you need here? I want to get back to Sydney and record this song." He wanted to push Vince onto his bed and lick across his shoulders, all the way down the ridges of his abdomen to the final prize. And yeah, his gaze dropped down to where Vince's cock stood to attention under the water. Those tight pants didn't hide anything.

"Yes. Let's go." Vince turned away, dove under the water, and swam away with long strokes. Just like the long strokes Riley wanted on his body with Vince's big hands exploring all of his skin. He breathed in deep, then pushed off the wall to swim after Vince, in pursuit of his touch.

13

Vince sat down in his office chair and closed his eyes. The last hour had been intense. Someone had told the press about Riley's movements and they'd been mobbed at the airport. Riley had carried it off like the pop star he was —with the practiced air of someone who'd done it all before —but the potential for a PR disaster hovered at the edges of Vince's calculations. He wasn't even sure what the disaster might be; they'd dealt with the rehab revelation quite well. There was one thing Vince hated more than anything— surprises. He wanted time to prepare his reaction to any situation and this fucking moment of being mobbed by tabloid journalists wasn't up there on his list of fun things. Riley's announcement to the press was so new and yes, they needed to take advantage of its currency before something else took over, but Vince also wanted to control Riley's appearances. He didn't appreciate the press knowing Riley's movements when he hadn't told them. He pressed his fingers to his temples to stop the beginnings of a headache. A light tap on his office door interrupted his contemplations.

"Come."

Uma walked in. "I found the leak." Ella and Anna followed her into his office and Ella closed the door behind them. For his lawyer and his PA to join her made sense, and Vince indicated that Uma should continue with a nod.

"Craig sent out an email to all our media contacts."

"I see." Vince's brain went into overdrive. Craig didn't have the authority to do that; he led the advertising team, not media relations. Some of his team had assisted with Riley's new brand, but that was it. Craig had better have a fucking good reason for overstepping the bounds of his role, not to mention the absolute bullshit of leaking Riley's whereabouts to the press. What the hell had he been thinking? This wasn't in the strategic plan. Right. Vince gritted his teeth. The rivalry between Craig and the Strategy Manager, Stu, might be part of this. Was Craig trying to throw Stu under the bus? If so, he was doing a bad job of it. Fucking office politics. He was trying to run a successful business here, not deal with the tantrums of grown men who ought to know better. Craig's priorities were all up the shit if he thought this was the best use of his time. He should just do the job he was hired to do.

"Vince?" Ella, his lawyer, spoke up.

"Yes."

"We need to have a wider discussion about Craig."

Vince lifted the glass of sparkling water on his desk and took a sip. "Okay?"

"He's the type of guy who thinks metoo is an overreaction and that people have no sense of humour when they tell him his rape jokes aren't funny." Anna confirmed something Vince had wondered about for a while. He'd noticed that Craig's proposed ad campaigns often went beyond the line of good humour into outright offensiveness, and it'd been more problematic lately. However, he always ended up with final campaigns that clients were happy with and weren't awful, so Vince had written the rest off as part of the brainstorming process. But what if it wasn't?

"There's more." Ella folded her arms and uncharacteristically, she let her gaze slid away from his. He preferred his staff to meet him head on—that's why he employed them—to tell him the hard news when it was needed. He didn't need yes men, he needed the truth no matter how ugly otherwise he couldn't make the right decisions for Kapow.

"What?" Vince growled. Trust was a two way street, and when his lawyer and his PA said Craig's behaviour was misogynistic and out of line, then he believed them both. Plus, their comments aligned with his own instincts and clarified something he'd been trying to put his finger on for a couple of months. Craig's recent ideas showed a lack of understanding of the marketplace. They'd sell stuff to bigots, but they also had the potential to blow up in their client's face. He'd let it slide though, because Craig always had good ideas among his proposals, and those were the ones that ended up being used. But the pattern remained.

"He called you a homophobic slur."

"I see." Vince didn't need anything else. Craig would be out of Kapow in the next hour. Yes, it might make him a hypocrite to sack him over something personal when the asshole had been harassing his staff for months. But then, if he'd known about the harassment when it had happened, he would've made this decision a long time ago. He couldn't act without knowledge.

"It just happened, and that's why we are here."

"Excuse me? You didn't think to open with that?"

The three woman cast their views down and he took in three deliberate breaths to slow the rising red mist behind his eyes.

"We thought the leak was more important." Uma lifted her face to stare at him and he nodded.

"It is. But how does that lead to the slur?"

"Technically, the slur lead to the leak."

He shut his eyes for a second, not wanting to shoot the messengers. "Explain. Please."

"A few minutes ago, a photo of you and Riley walking towards your rideshare car at the airport was posted on social media. It hasn't gone viral or anything, but Craig saw it and called you a pair of flaming—"

"Stop. I don't need to hear what he said." Vince's next question would be about Craig's contract and ensuring confidentiality when he sacked Craig. They'd have to redo everything he was working on, to avoid potential breaches of trust with clients, and he'd need to personally call every client that Craig had contact with recently. What a pain in the ass. But having people he trusted mattered more than the extra work it would create to get rid of Craig.

"Um, there's something else."

"Yes?" He aimed for relaxed and open but from the

wide-eyed stares on his employee's face, he wasn't sure he pulled it off.

"In the photo, you have your hand on Riley's waist. That's why Craig said that, but there's good news too." Uma rattled off the last section quickly and he waved his hand for her to continue. "You can't tell it's you in the photo. Your hat covers your face, but of course, we all recognised you."

"And it's a problem?" Obviously Vince didn't need the drama of having his relationship, or whatever it was, with Riley spread all over the internet. It might even be good for business to be seen together in the press. Gay marriage was legal now in Australia. Sixty percent of the country—those who voted in favour of gay marriage—would be happy for Riley, although he would've preferred to crunch the data on how many of those positive voters overlapped with Riley's fan base before the world realised that there might be something going on with Riley and himself. He was always more comfortable with a decision once he knew the data.

"Everyone on staff is cool with it, well those that have seen the photo anyway, and the people working on Riley's stuff just want you to be happy. Then Craig said that thing that you said not to repeat and when no one laughed, he said he was just kidding." Uma sounded flustered and he wanted to put her at ease, except his jaw ached from holding it shut. The implications of the photo had to wait. He had something more important to deal with first. Sacking Craig would be easy. The laws in Australia for unfair dismissal only applied to people earning under a certain sum, and given that Craig earned more than that, he could be out the door with no warning and no process.

They were good laws, protecting middle and low income earners from instant dismissal, but giving business the flexibility to get rid of expensive highly paid staff when they fucked up.

"He does that a lot you know," Uma continued, apparently unaware of the glowing rage surrounding Vince, unless she was aware and carried on regardless. Vince almost grinned; he liked his employees to be tough under pressure. "It's how he works out if people agree with him. He'll tell a joke, usually one that's vaguely sexist, to gauge people's response. If they laugh, then the next time, he'll tell another joke that's more offensive; racist or homophobic. And whenever someone tells him it's not funny, or people don't laugh, then he knows where their line is."

When Vince was younger, he would have applauded the strategy—not the bigotry—it was interesting from a psychological point of view as a way of figuring out who aligned with someone's views. Not anymore. He was too old and cynical to find the good in everyone. Some people didn't deserve that.

"I don't accept bigotry at Kapow. Thank you for telling me." Vince paced out of his office, leaving the three women behind. He opened the door, then turned back to the pair. "Ella. As of this moment, Craig is no longer employed by Kapow. Can you please start the process of removing him from the business? Come with me. Let's inform him now."

"Thank you, Vince. One other thing…"

"Yes?" What else?

"Do you want me to issue a takedown notice for that photo?"

Vince breathed out as he ran through the options.

"That's really up to our client. Ring Riley and ask him, although with the internet being what it is, it probably won't make any difference." He couldn't do everything and getting rid of Craig—and anyone in his team who sided with him— was more urgent than dealing with a photo that was already out there in the world. He stiffened. It wouldn't make any difference to leave the photo there. "Uma? Don't bother our client with this. Don't ask them to take down the photo. It'll only draw more attention to it. Inform Riley, and then come up with some strategies for our next step."

"Good idea. Let's control the narrative around it. I mean, the photo is pretty vague. A few people are shipping you with Riley—the whole bodyguard-client romance thing —but most comments seem to just be saying that it's good that Riley has someone to protect him from the sharks in the press."

"Right." Because two men couldn't possibly be lovers. The mental gymnastics people went through to explain away queer behaviour always astounded him. A simple explanation was usually better.

"Come on, Ella." As he walked along the hall towards Craig's office, he figured this would go one of two ways. Either Craig was joking and he didn't really mean it—bullshit—or he'd arc up and point to political correctness making his life impossible. Also bullshit. Neither would help him keep his job.

"Vince?"

"Ella." He tried not to sound exasperated.

"I hope you and Riley are happy."

Vince spun on his heels and glared at her. "Riley and I

are not anything. One casual moment of assistance to a client to protect them from the media means nothing. There is no Riley and I."

"But what about Craig?"

"Ella. I will not tolerate bigotry of any type at Kapow. Nor will I tolerate an employee leaking information to the press without my knowledge."

"Of course. Let's get this done." Ella opened the door to Craig's offices. His team had a large open plan room and Craig had a desk in the far corner. There was a glass walled meeting room if people needed to discuss anything in confidentiality, but Vince immediately decided he wasn't going to use it for this conversation. Everyone in Craig's team needed to know that they were gone if they agreed with Craig, and that Vince would protect them if they had been hurt by Craig.

He cleared his throat. "Attention, everyone." The response was instant, with chairs pushed back and heads swivelling to stare at him. The big boss. Good. He needed their full attention.

After the surge of press at the airport, Riley had been shuffled out of the rideshare car into the Kapow offices and been left in a meeting room while everyone had gone back to work. He'd popped down to his 4WD to grab a guitar, and he was quietly working on his new song when he heard a couple of doors banging. The song was missing something—that special factor that would take it from an angry rant into a song that would speak to people, that would make them grind in time with the beat, and expel all that negative energy. Ironically, the most recent time Riley had experienced that type of release, the one he needed the song to convey, was with Vince. He should observe him for a while and see if that would help unlock the last magical piece of creativity that this song required. He poked his head out of the meeting room, only to hear Vince blast his lawyer.

"There is no Riley and I."

Bullshit there wasn't. Not if the way Vince had guided him past the press only an hour ago was any marker with his hand possessively on Riley's back. His skin still tingled there, as if he'd been tattooed by Vince's protective presence. The way Vince stared hungrily at him in the pool, with his hard cock outlined through his barely present swimming trunks told the full story of his desire for Riley. "No Riley and I" was total crap. Was Vince embarrassed to be with him?

Riley closed the door to the meeting room with a quiet snick and picked up his guitar. He started to pick out a blues melody to reflect the rolling hurt in his gut, as if he'd eaten something that disagreed with him. Fucking Vince. He didn't have to be so pinpoint precise in his dismissal of their… well, whatever it was. It wasn't a relationship, but it was more than nothing. The pace of his fingers picked up on the fret board and his other hand strummed harder. Relentless. Yes, that's what he wanted. Never again. Never again. The lyrics came easily now that he had the rhythm sorted. That's what this song needed. A relentless melody, one that was unforgiving, one that took all the fury and frustration at being seen a certain way, at being forced to perform as the life and soul of the party while inside knowing that it was destroying him. This song would beat out a tempo that gave all of that to the audience. It didn't matter what they were annoyed about, this song would get them moving, dancing, jumping until sweat poured down their spines and their voices were hoarse from screaming the lyrics along with him. He could picture it now; himself on stage while thousands of people flung their arms in the air and joined their voices with his as they released all the power of this song into the world. *Never again. No one dictates my life to me. I am mine.* With one last hurrah, he ended the song and breathed out. Yes. That was it. He grabbed his phone and started a new recording with the new opening section, the bluesy intro, all soulful and almost teary, before it ramped up the energy into the chorus of the song. The crux of it. He couldn't wait to get this into a studio and layer it up with all the different parts. The drum beat, the bassline, everything adding into an almost operatic moment. Once he had the basic song down, then he'd know what else it needed. A touch of genius that would come from electronica, most likely. He pressed the button to stop recording and looked up, right at Vince who stood impossibly close to him.

"How long have you been standing here?"

"Not long. We have a small problem that you need to come and discuss."

Riley's pulse was still beating out the tune of his song. "Really? I'm employing you to deal with it."

"You'll want to be here for this one." Vince leaned so close that his lips brushed across Riley's ear. "We are being shipped by the internet."

"I thought there is no Riley and I." Riley sneered. Vince stood up straight, his expression fierce and if it wasn't for the slight colour on his cheeks, Riley would've assumed he didn't care.

"You heard that?"

Riley shrugged one shoulder. It didn't need a response.

"Right, obviously since you mention it." Vince scrubbed his hand over his jaw. "Look, at the airport someone took a photo of you getting in the car with my hand on your waist. There's nothing really in it, but—"

"We are being shipped as a couple." Riley shrugged, properly this time. "It's irrelevant. Let them. It happened all the time with So You Think. Or are you concerned about your own reputation?" It'd be a pretty shitty way to be outed, and all the vestiges of energy in Riley's pulse rate fled as he tried to send Vince a look that conveyed the sympathy he felt.

"So far, the internet has assumed I'm your bodyguard."

"Kind of true." Riley winked.

"More like your media bulldog."

A splutter of a laugh got caught between Riley's teeth. "So stern." And sexy.

"You are trouble."

"And you like it."

A rough growl was the only noise before Vince's lips covered his and Riley kissed him back with all the energy he'd put into his song. The guitar was an unwelcome barrier between them, digging into Riley's chest, but he barely noticed as Vince kissed him like he was fresh water after a long run.

Riley placed one hand on Vince's chest and pushed him away. "You liar."

"What?" Vince leaped backwards and stared at him, his brown eyes dark and unblinking.

"Either the kiss is a lie or us being nothing is a lie." Riley's voice cracked, unwittingly telling the truth when he'd meant it as a flirty joke. Vince's chest rose and fell a few times, then he blinked once. His gaze hardened and became calculated, as if he'd built an instantaneous barrier between them.

"We both have work to do. Get that song done, and I'll work out a strategy for the photo." He bolted from the room, and Riley groaned under his breath. Vince hadn't answered his question, and Riley couldn't tell if his chest hurt because the guitar had pressed into it, or because Vince didn't want him as much he'd hoped.

14

How dare Riley call him a liar? His entire brand was built on honesty, unlike a fucking washed up pop star who needed the money because he'd literally pissed his last opportunity against a wall. Vince jabbed the button to his private elevator and stepped inside. Bloody Riley and the way he fucked with his life. He couldn't keep doing this; wanting his body and his kisses, and never being able to trust anything he said. How fucking dare Riley call him a liar? He clenched his fist tighter, then forced himself to relax it. His father would've punched a wall by now, all fire and pointless fury, but Vince had too much control to let loose like that. There was only one cure for this burning rage in his blood. Angry sex.

No—not everything came back to Riley and the rush of chemistry between them. He'd been transfixed by watching Riley play his guitar; he was the wild bird in a tree who could never be caged. Standing inside the door to the meeting room, Vince had understood why Riley needed to play and to share his music. The idea of him staying in a small town without spreading his wings and showing the world his talent, his beauty, and his song cut at Vince, and he had let himself get caught up in the music. There were a few threads that reminded him of that old bloody So You Think CD that had been stuck in his car all those years ago, and it blended with something new and more mature. There was skill and talent in the way Riley coaxed the guitar to make sounds that conveyed all that emotion, and Vince knew he wanted to be a larger part of Riley's life. He selfishly wanted Riley to write a song about him; about them. And wasn't that a joy and a curse?

Until Riley ruined the moment by calling Vince a liar. His ears filled with a roar that drowned out everything else, and he'd known right then that the curse of Riley would always be more than any joyful moments. He had to get away. He needed to run. He'd pound the pavement until he couldn't breathe anymore; that's what it would take to rid his body of Riley. He needed to push himself until he could think properly without this swirl of uncertainty coursing in his veins. He wanted to regain his legendary calm control over his environment—the one thing he'd spent years creating—and he hated how Riley made him feel like he sat poised on the edge of a cliff, ready to fall.

He swiped into his apartment, threw on some running clothes and shoes, then began his run by going down the stairwell. All the way from the penthouse to the ground floor. Liar. Liar. The word clanged with every step. If anyone was a liar, it was the addict. Not him. Vince pushed open the fire door and stepped out in the city streets. Sydney in the week before Christmas was usually dry and warm, and he dragged the hot air into his lungs but compared to the dusty air in Bourke, it was almost humid. Sultry. An acrid hint of bushfire smoke clung to the general city smell, over the notes of car fumes, rubbish, and general grime that mingled with coffee and hundreds of different types of food from the greasy perfume of chip shops to the sharpness of fried garlic. None of the scents were quite as distinctive as burning gum trees. He launched into a run, even though he wasn't really feeling the same urgency as before. His rage never lasted long; it screamed and then was done, and he'd long ago learned how to control the first burst of it, so he always gave others the impression of calm. Simply running down all those stairs had been enough to dissipate the worst of it. Now he was on the street, the noise in his ears had died down to a hum, and he headed down to the Opera House to join the legions of ultra-fit financiers going for the lunchtime run. He settled into a rhythm; those same financiers were the ones who purchased the products Kapow pedalled for clients.

Sweat dripped down his spine as he ran, his legs pounding the pavement and his arms swinging steadily. He went past the steps of the Opera House and ran into the Botanic Gardens with the harbour to his left. The bitumen path shimmered with reflected heat—to go for a run at the peak of the day's heat was an absurd decision—but he deserved the hurt in his muscles because he'd already made the bad decision of saying yes to Riley's body. Riley had been the one to suggest they fuck to get rid of their lust. To blame Riley would be dishonest—his pride in his honesty wouldn't allow him to do that—Vince had said yes with his eyes open, knowing that once wouldn't be enough. He'd even bypassed his own caution to be involved with an addict for the sake of lust. It pulled him towards Riley with a force of its own, one that overrode all good sense. He picked up the pace as he turned and went up the hill back towards the city. Yes, that was it. Lactic acid burned in his muscles now and his lungs begged for more oxygen. He needed to remember his life goals and stop letting Riley get in his way.

A couple of hours later, after a shower, a very late lunch, and dressed in a fresh suit, Vince was ready to head back to work. Most of his staff would be finishing up for the day soon and he'd have the office to himself to do all the work he hadn't done today because he'd been too frustrated to think. It wasn't precisely a lie to call all this negative energy irritation. He was annoyed that this situation with Riley tore his focus away from work and his core goals. Damn pesky feelings. Ella stopped him in the hallway and confirmed that Craig was gone, and a light wave fresh air ruffled his hair. His goals were on track and he nodded to Anna as he thanked Ella then walked past Anna's desk into his office.

"Are you alright, Vince?" Anna shuffled from one foot to the other, hovering in the doorway.

"Yes."

"It's just that you, um, disappeared after sacking Craig

and I just wanted to say… Well, thank you for listening to us."

"It's fine." Shit, had that been today? What a day. No wonder he felt wrecked. He picked up a pen, rather than rub his eyes.

"It's more than fine. Not every boss would listen to a PA over someone as senior as Craig."

"I'm not every boss."

Anna nodded vigorously, like one of those bobble head dolls people put in the back of their cars. "Yes, well, thank you. Is there anything you need?"

"No."

"Okay." Anna turned around and left him alone with the depressing realisation that he'd done the bare minimum to resolve a crap situation and he was being praised, uplifted, for it. The bar for decent behaviour was far too low if Anna and Ella thought he was special for sacking a bigot like Craig. An acidic tang washed over his tongue; it was worse than that because he'd suspected for too long before he'd acted. That they praised his tardy efforts was a sad reflection on what they had to cope with in their everyday lives. On that note… Vince flung open his office door.

"Anna?"

"Yes."

"Is Riley still here?"

Anna frowned. "I'm not sure. I mean, I didn't see him leave, but if he did, he might not tell me anyway. Shall I ring him for you?"

"No, it's fine. It can wait." Or rather, he could put off his apology. During his shower, he'd run back over their conversation and realised he'd over-reacted to Riley's comment. Riley hadn't called him a liar, not really, he'd only pointed out the disparity between his actions and his words. He paced back into his office and sat down at his desk to stare blankly at his emails. One gorgeous man and a few amazing kisses shouldn't derail him like this. He'd fucked plenty of men and never had this response, yet the concept of going out there and sleeping with someone who wasn't Riley hit like a hammer to the sternum. Nope. He stretched his shoulders and neck. It was time to stop sweating on this, put his head down and get some work done. The door opened and in walked Riley, as if he'd summoned him by thinking about him. Ha, Riley had been in his thoughts all day in one form or another. No amount of trying to avoid him had worked, so he may as well confront Riley head on. It was more his style than all this pointless internal cyclical argument.

"You were looking for me?"

"I take it Anna mentioned that." Vince stood and drew himself to his full height.

"Is this about work?"

"Yes." Vince couldn't keep being distracted by Riley.

"Okay? What? Has something happened with that photo?"

"The photo? Oh, no. Uma hasn't given me an update, so I assume it's all been forgotten already."

"Then?" Riley had a puzzled expression. Vince opened his mouth to start, then slammed his lips shut as the word Liar taunted him.

"You look like you are begging for an argument."

"Don't you mean gagging for an argument?" Vince cursed himself—the last thing he needed was an image of Riley sucking on his cock until he gagged. Shit.

"Whatever. What happened and why are you so pissed about it?"

"There can be no more kisses between us. It has to end."

"Okay?" Riley cocked his head to the side as if considering whether to say more.

"You said yourself that it was a one time thing. And now it's done." Vince spotted the beginnings of a smile on Riley's face before he hid his mouth with his hand.

"Now I think you are lying." Riley shifted his hand and held it out in a stop gesture. "Not to me, to yourself."

"No. Kissing you is the lie. You said I had a choice and I choose work. I always will." Vince's skin crawled as he pushed Riley away.

"Right? The kiss or nothing?"

"It's going to have to be nothing." Damn, that sounded too much like a question, not a statement.

Riley raised one eyebrow, then slowly nodded. "Fine. But I deserve to know why you are pushing me away. What we have is good. Powerful, even."

"It's not because it's false. You are only chasing a high. It's temporary and it can't go any further."

Riley took a half-step backwards, a deep frown between his eyebrows. "Hold on a damned second. Did you just say that I'm chasing a high? Are you referring to my past as an addict?"

Vince crossed his arms. "Once an addict, always an addict. That behaviour will never change."

RENÉE DAHLIA

"Wow. I didn't expect you would be quite so fucking judgemental. I've been sober for eight years. People can change and I have."

"Not in my experience."

"And that is?"

"Nothing."

Riley scoffed. "Oh come on now. You want an argument and you want to judge me but you won't give me the whole story? That's bullshit."

"Fine. My father was an addict." For some reason, Vince's lungs hurt as if his own breath scalded him. He never told anyone about that and here he was blurting out the secrets of his past to Riley when he'd much rather never think about that time ever again. He'd spent the last decade working to erase the worst of his past and rebuild what had been lost.

"I'm not your father."

"But you are an addict and all addicts are the same."

Riley shook his head. His eyes shone and Vince looked away not wanting to see the pity he knew would be written all over Riley's face. "If that's what you think, then you right. There is no future between us. I'm going to get in my 4WD now and head back to Bourke. Let me know when you next need me for an interview or whatever."

Vince's heart stopped beating. "Wait." He couldn't let Riley leave.

"Mate." The warning in Riley's voice should've been enough for Vince to leave it alone. Having Riley walk away was what he wanted, except, no, he wanted it on his terms.

"Please." Vince never begged—not that Riley would

142

know that—and his stomach churned like milk and lemon juice. "I've built my brand on honesty and…"

"It's pretty bloody dishonest to lump all addicts together and assume everyone's journey is the same."

"I…" Fuck. He hated this uncertainty. It made his skin crawl and he didn't know what to do about it, a cycle that could only be solved by being brazen and laying down the truth as he saw it. "Fine. I'll tell you what I know and what I see. My grandfather came to Australia as a poor migrant after the war and he worked his butt off to become Australia's first billionaire. That's my legacy, that's what I am achieving here."

"What has that got to do with addiction? Although one might argue being a workaholic is a type of addiction." Riley's light hearted sing song voice raised the hairs on Vince's arms and he crossed them tight across his aching chest.

"Not at all the same. A workaholic builds something. An addict, like my father, took everything Nonno, I mean my grandfather, built and destroyed it. By the time I was fifteen it was all gone, spent on parties and drugs and countless trips to rehab."

"Like I said, everyone's journey is different and not everyone beats their addiction the first time."

Vince sneered. "He didn't even try. When Nonno was alive, he'd force my father into rehab but Pa would just run away. And then as soon as Nonno died, my useless father sold the whole business and put the proceeds up his nose. He lived as an addict and he died as one."

"If you think I'm anything like that, then you are right.

It's best we end this now before it matters to either of us." Riley walked out of Vince's office with a controlled calm that Vince envied, even as he took the hit to his jugular. He couldn't even revel in being right because Riley had beaten him to it. He let out a deflating breath before he dragged in a deep one. There was only one thing to do when life didn't go your way. Get to work and build a new, better, stronger, path to success. He didn't need Riley for that. Hard work would get rid of this crushing sensation in his chest. It had to; he had nothing else.

15

Riley stood in the carpark at Kapow and reminded himself that the biggest risk he took when uploading his Riley Le Breton tunes had nothing to do with the music. People would either love it, hate it, or have no emotional connection to it at all. He couldn't control their reactions to his songs. All he could do was make the best music he could with a focus on continual improvement. The marketing catch-phrase—continual improvement—made the muscle in his jaw clench for a second. Three weeks ought to have been enough to forget how Vince made him feel; the crackle of chemistry between them, the roughness of his fingertips gliding over his skin, the way his cock filled his mouth, and the taste of him. Salt and spice. Apparently it wasn't long enough but he was old enough and wise enough to know better than to chase someone who couldn't grow the fuck up and realise that all addicts weren't the same. It still burned, bitter at the back of his throat, whenever he remembered the argument and the way Vince crossed his arms and sneered at him. Riley was better off without someone who didn't respect the effort he'd made to change, and to stay sober.

Which, of course, was the real problem with tonight's cocktail event. He'd be surrounded by alcohol and worse, by people offering it to him all the time. There was a real risk that he'd forget about the music and get caught up in the lifestyle of being a pop star. Tonight would be his first time back in that world, under the spotlight of the music industry, and at a party, a place where people would expect to see the Riley Micah of old with all the expectations to be the life of the party. It was literally in the name of the event—cocktail party—and he couldn't avoid it because several people in attendance would be good for promoting his new album once it was completed. If he wanted to get global reach, beyond one article by Stella Michaels, he had to attend. It would test his resolve, and yet, three weeks after the argument with Vince, his mind was absorbed by thoughts of Vince rather than being stressed about how he'd cope tonight.

He missed him. It was illogical because Vince had made his position clear. The temptation to try and show Vince that he was nothing like Vince's father beckoned every day, yet Riley knew enough about addiction and the impacts on addict's families that it would be pointless to push Vince. Besides, he was proud of his journey and he wasn't going to change himself for someone who wanted to throw him into an ugly box that he didn't fit inside. He was nothing like Vince's father for one simple reason. He gotten help when he'd needed it and he'd done the work to change his habits. Riley couldn't force Vince to see the difference, he'd have to come to that realisation on his own. If only it didn't disappoint him so much. He'd really thought they'd had a proper connection, but it was all built on posturing and lust which was not a solid base for a relationship. Damn. This hurt so deeply because despite his initial proposal, he had wanted a relationship with Vince. He'd grown to respect him and wanted to spend more time with him. Now it was dead in the water, he didn't have to think about how they would've made the practical stuff work. Vince was too focused on his business to travel with Riley when he toured. Touring his soon to be released, still unnamed, album would be the next natural step in creating a career from Riley Le Breton. Maybe it was for the best that they had realised they weren't compatible now before they had to figure out logistics. Yeah, nah.

Lingering outside the elevator at the Kapow offices wasn't going to resolve anything either. He shook out his hands, pressed the button, and stepped inside. The lift carried him quickly upwards, and when the doors opened, he signed in at the front desk, then walked down the hallway towards Vince's office ready for the pre-event meeting. Ready? No, but he could fake it. Probably. He wasn't going to be the guy who slunk back to the country because he couldn't hack it in the big smoke. He'd done all of this before and had been a huge success before he'd fucked it up. This time, he knew what he wanted, and he was determined to take his old experiences and use them as a guide for a new success. He had creative control over Riley Le Breton and that was the perfect motivation for finding a way to cope with an event that would push all his triggers. He'd literally employed Kapow Advertising to give him control over the business of Riley Le Breton. It would be fine.

"Hey Riley, it's so good to see you again. How's the album going?" Anna's enthusiasm did nothing for the swirling breeze in his gut. Later tonight, it'd probably turn into a tornado. Damn, stop thinking about that. He really didn't need to borrow trouble from the future, as his Mama always said. Later tonight, he'd simply keep his hands busy by holding a bottle of water and he'd network.

"It's going well. Thanks for asking."

"You've been in Bourke the whole time?"

Riley chuckled. "I do live there. So yeah. Plus the high school has an excellent studio set up that I can use for recording. It's pretty sweet for a country town."

"Do we get to hear any new songs before you release them?"

"Sure."

Anna squealed and a huge grin stretched over her face. "So cool."

"I've recorded Never Again as well as two others; Barely a Moment, and Sunday Silence." A hit of endorphins filled his body in a rush that mirrored her enthusiasm. He couldn't wait to be on stage performing these for an audience, especially Never Again with its thumping beat.

"Awesome. I've had your early stuff on repeat. The boss made me put headphones on to listen to them though."

"Did he now?" Riley couldn't help but wonder if Vince banned his music because he was mad at him, or because he missed him too. Ah, that was probably too much to hope after their last conversation. If he'd missed him, he might have called. Instead, Riley had spent more time talking to Anna and Uma about his marketing plans; well, anything was more than zero.

"He said something about endless pop being too repetitive."

"Anna. You make me sound so old." Vince's voice flowed over Riley's skin and he wanted to shut his eyes and drink it in. "Oh, Riley you are here. Come into my office and we can discuss the plan for tonight." He'd disappeared again before Riley had the chance to react. It took him a moment to stop feeling so stunned. He had expected a little more reaction from Vince after so long away, but there hadn't been a flicker on his poker face. It was like someone had taken all the rampaging chemistry from the last time they'd met and buried it deeper than a diamond mine, never to be noticed again.

"Are you okay?"

"Yeah, just..." Just trying to figure out that reaction from Vince. "Um, does he have ... ahhh ... a thing on your desk so he knows what you are saying?" Riley didn't mean it in quite such a creepy way, but damn, Vince couldn't have just known he was standing there chatting to Anna.

"Nah. I sent him a text when you walked up to my desk so he'd know you were here for your meeting. It's, like, my job."

"Cool. That makes a lot more sense." It also meant that Vince had had time to prepare for seeing him, so perhaps he wasn't as unaffected as he appeared. Wishful fucking thinking, Riley. Hell. He'd written two songs for Vince, pouring his angst into the tunes, and the man didn't even have the decency to look bothered by his presence.

Anna laughed. "I don't know what they teach you in the country about working in an office, but Vince is totally not a creepy boss. Trust me on that one." There was obviously more to that story, given the passionate defence of Vince in Anna's tone, but Riley didn't want to press her for more details. He really didn't need to hear about Vince's heroics right now. If Vince wanted to keep his distance and treat him like a terrible addict who would ruin everyone's lives, then he guessed that was his only option now. Put Vince— and the way his touch made Riley's skin light up—into a box and throw it away forever, in the dark where judgemental pricks belonged.

"Okay." Riley blew out an unsteady breath. The Riley of So You Think would've marched into Vince's office and made a joke to dust away the tension between them. Now he was over a decade older, presumably wiser, the concept stuck in his throat like a chicken bone. Vince had been incredibly precise about why he didn't want to spend any more time with him, and there was really no comeback for the truths he'd told. But Riley missed him and seeing a snippet of him and having his voice reverberate over his skin for a moment only made his yearning stronger. He missed Vince's kisses, his spectacular body, and most of all, he missed the way Vince was so bloody cute when he wasn't being the boss of the world. Riley liked the cocky side of Vince too—more than a little bit—but there was a realness whenever Riley got to peek behind the confident facade. He wanted to change that first rule they'd set when they'd met;

he wanted more than a quick fuck to get rid of chemistry. The original plan hadn't worked because his body bloody nearly glowed in Vince's presence. It always had and with hindsight, any expectation that this wild chemistry would dissipate after one or two kisses seemed like wishful thinking.

"I'd better go to our meeting." He pushed open the door, slowly, to see Vince pacing back and forth as he spoke on the phone in another language. The strength of his charisma was like a bright aura around him—more than surface deep—as he fluently convinced whoever was on the other end of the call to do whatever Vince wanted them to do. Riley had no clue as to the words spoken. Vince moved with conviction and confidence and that gave the impression that Vince would get everything he wanted. Riley knew what it was like to have all of that focused on him and he missed it with a sudden tug in his gut. Was it only a month ago that he'd had his interview with Triple J and he'd propositioned Vince in the parking garage? It seemed like longer, or perhaps this yearning was merely because he wanted longer with Vince; more time to understand why he wore supreme confidence like a safety blanket, as if he could wrap himself up from the world by being better than everyone else.

"Sorry about that."

"It's okay. What language were you speaking?" Yeah, good work, Riley. He opened with an innocuous question rather than the rehearsed apology for dismissing Vince's concerns.

"Cantonese."

"Like Hong Kong?" Riley couldn't help but be impressed.

"Yes. I spent a year there as part of my business degree. It's the core business hub of the Asia-Pacific region, and at the time I thought it would be an asset to me."

"And is it?"

"Absolutely." Vince sat on the edge of his desk. "Did you want something?"

Yes, he wanted Vince and the chance to try and make this physical connection into a proper relationship. He wanted more than lust. Riley cleared his throat. Wanting Vince was hopeless when he wasn't ready to accept Riley as he was. "You, or technically Uma on your behalf, told me I had to be here for a pre-event meeting. I'm here. What do you want to talk about?"

"Look, it's not really a big deal. I've been to several of these Christmas parties in the last couple of weeks. Mostly it's people standing around drinking champagne and talking."

Riley rolled his eyes. "Vince. I used to be a pop star on the global stage. It might have been a few years since I entertained crowds and went to music industry parties, but I do know how this works."

"Hence why I said it was no big deal." Vince's terse tone told Riley that it really was a big deal, but if Vince wanted to lambast him over his old drinking addiction, he should just say so.

"Why are we bothering with this meeting if you aren't going to impart anything useful?" Riley had driven to Sydney yesterday and hadn't slept that well in his hotel room last night because of this meeting. And now it was a waste of his time. All the previous hope he'd built up in his mind fled like a cat who'd been shot with a water pistol. Bitterness at having wasted his time on someone who didn't want to see the real him made his tongue all furry and gross, the bad taste of old coffee, and he wanted to brush his teeth and replace it all with mint.

"Hold on." Vince swiped his thumb over his phone and called someone. "Uma. Come to my office. … Thanks."

Silence filled the room, thick and awkward.

"Vince, I know you have concerns about my history with addiction and I'm guessing tonight is some sort of test for you."

"Not true. Uma organised tonight because it's a good chance to get you in front of a bunch of local media."

Riley glared sarcastically at Vince. "I'm sure that is some of the truth."

"Accusing me of lying isn't going to get you anywhere."

"Perhaps if you were honest with yourself to start with, we wouldn't be having this standoff."

"Nothing in that statement is true."

Riley shook his head. "We aren't having a standoff? Or you are dishonest with yourself? Mate."

"You aren't my mate."

"No, but I've been your lover and I much prefer that."

Vince's nostrils flared and his jaw tightened so the muscles at the corners hardened. "A one night stand doesn't make a lover." His voice dropped in volume and somehow that was more intimidating than if he'd yelled, except Riley's blood pumped rapidly and he squared his shoulders, ready to fight back, or kiss him, because damn, Vince was so hot when he glared like that.

"Now who is the liar? What we had was more than one night and you know it." Riley sneered and held up his palm. "But you know what? If you want to push me away, then that's your prerogative."

There was a single knock on the door, then Uma walked in. She stopped in the middle of the room, her gaze flicking between the two of them. Riley's lungs burned as he aimed for calming breaths, and Vince's cheeks had red slashes across them. At least he wasn't as unaffected as he said he was.

"Are you two okay? It's not about that pesky photo, is it? I really thought that would've died down by now."

"Photo?"

"OMG, didn't I tell you? There's fan fiction out there now about Riley Micah and his hot bodyguard." Uma grinned; her good humour completely at odds with the wicked tension that swirled around Riley. He wanted to finish fighting with Vince and then maybe kiss the fuck out of him. So much for finding peace with the way Vince had ended things three weeks ago.

"It's pretty amazing, actually. I've been wondering if we should contact some of the authors and talk about using it for promotional material, but then, I don't really like the idea of bouncing off internet ships for marketing. It feels weird, somehow."

"Seventy-two percent of Riley's So You Think fans are okay with him being gay, but I'm not sure that's enough support to build a marketing strategy around." Vince's voice was tightly wound.

"We've worked with less, but I'm not sure it's what we want. It takes the story away from the music, and there is enough in Riley's life doing that already. That's why tonight's Christmas cocktail party is the perfect one for Riley to attend. Most of the Australian music industry will be there, music bloggers, radio hosts, and of course media. They'll all get to see him and talk to him and he can show how excited he is about his new album."

"I wouldn't have driven all the way from Bourke for just any dinner. I did read your emails, Uma." Riley swallowed down the bitterness as he held back the full truth. He'd come for Vince too, to see if there was a chance they could reignite the connection between them. It was a long bloody drive for the off chance that Vince might have spent the last three weeks figuring out that all addicts were not the same. It seemed he'd wasted his time, but he could still make the most of this evening and talk to as many media contacts as possible. He wouldn't be the wild Riley of old. He'd just be himself; older and less intimidated by the situation he'd ended up in. He didn't need a social crutch anymore. He'd earned his place this time—he was more than a pretty face with great vocal chords —he'd written this music and it was all him. Not manufactured like his last time around this particular block. Yes, he'd beaten six thousand applicants to earn his spot in So You Think. He'd earned that, and yet, he'd been the heady young mix of cocky and an imposter in a glamourous world, trying to belong.

"Awesome. What are you going to wear?"

"A tuxedo." Vince interjected in that gorgeous commanding tone of his. Riley wished he didn't want Vince so much; this rowdy swirl of emotion rushing between hurt and lust would likely give him a headache.

"I'm a pop star, not a businessman. I could wear ripped jeans and a leather jacket with nothing underneath and no one would blink."

"I don't think that would help with the rumours around your sexuality."

Riley's eyebrows shot up so fast, it almost hurt. "I can clarify those rumours with one tweet. I'm not ashamed of who I am. Uma, you can tell the world that I'm bisexual and—"

"Careful." Vince's warning bounced off him.

"And I'm currently not in a relationship. If you want to address that photo of my bodyguard… Actually, don't bother. Just leave it be."

Uma nodded. "What do you think Vince?"

"The data says he'll have support if he says that. There will be bigots of course, but you know my position on that."

Riley wanted Vince to elaborate on his position, and did his reluctance mean he wasn't actually out? Riley had just assumed and maybe he shouldn't have done that. His legs wobbled under him. Could it be that Vince was using his addiction as an excuse to stay safe? Riley stiffened. No, Vince had made his position very clear and anything else was merely wishful thinking on Riley's part.

"Yes. Okay. I'll sort that out before you arrive at the party. We have two hours to get Riley to wardrobe and sort out his clothes and set up some social media shots," said Uma.

"Excellent. You can escort Riley and I'll meet you there. And Uma, have you spoken to the organisers about Riley's sobriety?"

"Of course."

Riley wanted to stamp his feet. He wasn't a child who needed to be pandered to. "I can take care of myself. I've been doing it for eight years in a country town where alcohol greases all the social wheels."

"We are responsible for your image. It behoves us to ensure the environments we send you into are safe and inclusive."

"I see." Riley hated that office speak version of Vince. It was so clinical and removed. He wanted to do something childish—no, spontaneous—and kiss Vince on the cheek to see how he'd react. He needed to see the open truth behind the gruff mask.

"Come on, Riley. Let's get your outfit sorted." Uma waved towards the door. He glanced once more at Vince's stony expression, then left the room. Uma led him to the front of the building.

"Where are we going?"

"Shopping."

"Okay?"

"We don't exactly have a whole wardrobe in our offices just in case we need to dress a pop star. There is a huge mall only one block away. We'll start there. Are you happy to go with an upmarket version of what you wore to the last interview with Stacey Michaels? Those photos looked amazing and her article was a brilliant reintroduction to the world of music. We've had so many requests for interviews since then."

Riley hadn't been told about those and Uma's enthusiasm was a good reminder about why he'd hired a marketing company to look after that side of things. He'd much rather make more music than waste his time looking over emails and making decisions that would likely affect his sales.

"Most of them didn't have enough followers so we've declined them, but there are a couple of sources we are negotiating with. One will be here tonight, by the way, so we'd been sort out this outfit."

"Tight jeans, t-shirt. Sure."

"I think we can find a jacket to throw over that, and I'm thinking—"

"Stop. It's Christmas in Sydney. It's way too hot for a jacket. Nah, just a cute Christmas t-shirt and green jeans."

"Yeah that would work." Uma paused. "Hey, Riley?"

"Yeah?"

"How is Bryce?"

"He's good. You two really connected that day, didn't you?" Riley hadn't really talked to his flatmate about Uma; they'd both been busy with work getting ready for the Christmas/New Year shutdown. Riley had handed his notice in to Jordy, and his last day was next week. And when he wasn't at work, he was at the school working on recording more songs and improving the ones he'd already bedded down.

Uma nodded. "It's complicated though."

"Long distance is pretty tough, huh."

"Something like that. He's been thinking about asking you if you can stay flatmates when you move to the city."

"Absolutely." Riley hadn't decided if he was going to move back to Sydney, but if Bryce wanted to, then it'd be amazing to have a mate close by.

"Can you tell him… no, never mind. Let's get you dressed." Uma paced up the street, leaving Riley in her wake. Now he had a couple of hours to find something to wear that would tempt Vince, because apparently he was a masochist who couldn't walk away. Vince was so sure that Riley would fail tonight, that one addict was just like another. Nope. He would show him how wrong his assumptions were. Riley would attend tonight's party; he'd be sexy, he'd smile and talk about his music, and he'd do it all without artificial help. He breathed out; it wasn't as easy as simply declaring it to be.

16

Vince stepped out of his rideshare car and walked to the entrance. This was the fourth Christmas event he'd been to this week. It was that time of year when everyone wanted a party and all the parties blurred together, especially the client dinners, although this one promised to be interesting as there were potential new clients everywhere. He'd been working with Stu putting together some strategic plans for growing the PR arm of Kapow and tonight was the perfect opportunity to put out some feelers.

"Vince. So good to see you." Jamie tucked her arm in his. Her father Mr Cleveland owned Cleveland Marketing and was his biggest rival. For years they'd been careful to keep each at just the right distance when the cameras were focused on them. It was useful sometimes to have a beautiful woman on his arm especially when talking to clients with certain beliefs, and it was also convenient for her to have the pretence of a relationship with him in this cutthroat business. They'd become good friends, allies, in this game of public perception.

Ever since he'd met Riley, he'd started to care that he'd been holding back the truth about his sexuality for years now. Initially it had too much of a risk for his business, especially in the early years, and now it was a habit. Ironically, the advertising industry had a high proportion of queer people doing creative work, and he really should've felt freer to be himself before now. The realisation, on seeing Jamie, that he'd never been completely honest in public meant he'd have to acknowledge that he might be wrong about Riley's sobriety. And if he was wrong about that, he couldn't use it as an excuse to protect himself. The realisation clubbed him over the head. He'd told himself it was no one's business who he fucked and now he'd met someone he wanted to be seen in public with, he had to come to terms with the barriers he'd put up to prevent himself from rejection.

"How are you?" He'd spent years focused on building Kapow Advertising into a successful business platform to avenge the loss of his grandfather's wealth. His father had rejected him over and over and this success would be his revenge. But it felt hollow without someone—Riley—to share it with.

"I'm doing alright. It's been an age!" Jamie leaned closer and her cloying perfume surrounded him. He tried not to sneeze. "I have a slightly awkward question for you."

"Ask away. We are friends, aren't we?"

"If you can call a mutually beneficial media presence a friendship, then yes."

Vince smiled, almost laughing at the way she had their relationship down pat. No wonder he had a lot of time for her. "We do look great together in a photo and it benefits both Kapow and your father's business. Please, ask me your question."

She came even closer, and he could feel her eyelashes against his ear. Flashes of light from cameras surrounded them. "Did you really sack Craig?"

"Yes, I sacked him for harassing my employees. I won't stand for that behaviour."

"Oh." She blinked rapidly, her long eyelashes batting against his ear. With the media watching on, he couldn't react or leap away. "I think I'm in a lot of trouble."

"Your father won't help?"

"No. You know what he's like. He says he'll employ Craig if the rumours are true, but it's more than that. Father thinks we should marry."

"I take it your father doesn't know that Craig is already married." Vince's heart broke for her. What a bloody mess.

Jamie swallowed. "He is?"

Shit. "Yes. I'm sorry."

"But I'm pregnant. Father is going to kill me." There had been rumours in the advertising industry for years that Mr Cleveland beat up his wife and daughter, but Vince had dismissed them as the usual jealous nonsense between competing firms. He really needed to stop that; he'd already messed up by ignoring the issues around Craig and now this. When Jamie had an affair with Stu years ago, he'd deliberately gotten to know her because he didn't trust her father not to use her as a way of getting information from Stu. But she'd been open about how Mr Cleveland wanted her to marry a shareholder in Kapow—preferably him—to join the businesses together. Jamie was a complex person with a stronger set of ethics than her father, and they'd used each other for mutual gain. When Stu had fallen in love with his wife, Poppy, Jamie hadn't reacted well, and Vince had distanced himself from the whole mess.

Vince slung his arm around her waist. "He's not. I won't let him. I'll put you up in a hotel until you figure out what you want to do. Tonight. Don't mess around and stay in his house because he's going to find out sooner or later." He should've stayed her friend when things were tough rather than side with Stu and he might have been able to prevent this drama with Craig.

"Thank you. I'm so sorry to do this to you."

Regret was only useful if he used it to find solutions. "Please don't be sorry. Craig did this. Your father did this. We will find a solution."

"Thank you. I wish we could have… Well, that's never going to happen now."

Vince shook his head. "It's not you, Jamie. Surely, you'd figured that out by now."

"Oh."

"Let's talk about it later when there are less eyes on us. Right now, we are going to plaster on big smiles and go inside and pretend nothing is wrong. The best revenge on Craig, if that's what you want, is to be beautiful and successful."

Jamie stood up straight and smiled. "Let's do it."

The evening rushed by, filled with social chit chat, and several brilliant pieces of networking. He deliberately kept to the other side of the room than Riley who spent the party surrounded by people with Uma by his side. Not that Vince was keeping an eye on him or anything...

"Vince, this is Dylan Wilson. Dylan; Vince is my PR manager." Riley appeared at Vince's side to introduce a handsome blonde man with stunning blue eyes. He was vaguely familiar, and Vince stared at him as he tried to recall the man.

"Hi." He was usually good at faces and names but this one kept eluding him. Damn it.

"Dylan was in So You Think and now is a composer and producer for our old record label."

Fuck—that's where he knew him from—all the old promotional photos of the band that they'd gone through while designing Riley's website. "I had your album when I was younger."

"You did?" Riley asked. "You never mentioned that?"

"The best PR managers are fans." Dylan shared a glance with Riley that illuminated their history together and a rush of agony swarmed in his stomach like a wasp had been trapped there.

"Vince is not a fan of mine." Riley's tone was sharp enough to cut Vince's flesh.

"Ouch. But he just said he had one of our albums. Which one?"

"The one with Street Cry on it."

"Justify." Riley and Dylan spoke together.

"Hang on, you had the album but you don't recall what it was called? What sort of fan are you?" Dylan asked.

"This is where I admit I didn't buy the album. It came with a car I owned."

"And you just played it?"

Vince cleared his throat. He shouldn't have started this because it didn't really paint him in a great light. "Not on purpose. It was stuck in the CD player and just played on repeat over and over, like a demon cursed machine."

"Must have been a shit car!" Riley's grin lit up his face and Vince couldn't look away from his mouth. Desire shot up his spine and he tried to counter it by reminding himself that Riley was an addict who wouldn't stick around for him, but the thought faded away quickly.

"It's a good thing we had excellent music." Dylan's comment disappeared into background noise and he had to clear the thickness from his throat so he could stay focused on the conversation.

"Yeah, could've been worse. At least the car had brilliant fuel efficiency."

Dylan chuckled. "Hey, well good to meet you, Vince the accidental fan. I need to catch someone before they leave. Later, Riley."

"Fuel efficiency?" Riley raised one eyebrow. "Even when you were poor, you were all about the money."

Vince had never understood the phrase to get your back up until now. "Is that why you think I'm here?" He wouldn't lie to himself—he was here because he was greedy—he wanted more than money from Riley. The only question he had was one of risk, and this wasn't something he could find the answer to in a spreadsheet.

"It's why I hired you, so I shouldn't be so surprised."

Thank fuck. He could keep this about work. "And I'm worth every cent."

"I've had rather more than I initially bargained for." Riley's gaze slid down Vince's torso, searing him as if it were his tongue travelling that path, lingering for a couple of seconds on Vince's groin. His cock responded, swelling in anticipation.

"I've been watching you all evening."

"Creepy." Riley grinned.

Vince's cheeks burst with heat. "Fuck, Riley."

"Well, honestly. Who says that? You've been watching me because it's your job or because you're a creepy guy?" The tilted head, and the heat in Riley's gaze, all pointed to a tease, and yet, Vince couldn't quite let himself enjoy the moment.

"It's my job. I just wanted to compliment you for how well you've dealt with tonight."

"You mean because I'm an addict and you are surprised that I haven't broken eight years of sobriety. Because addicts never change, right?"

Vince wanted to pull his hair out. "I'm trying to apologise." He stumbled over the sentence. It wasn't something he had a lot of practice at.

"And doing a bang up job of it, mate. Just say it. I'm sorry I assumed you were a deadbeat loser like my father was and that I said a bunch of shit that was plainly wrong."

"Yeah, all of that."

Riley's eyebrows raised up and he shook his head slowly. "It's been three weeks, Vince, with absolutely no communication from you. It's obvious that you don't really want this, so how about we just leave it be? I'm happy to work with Uma from now on."

Vince hated this. He always knew what to do and what to say. It felt like his brain and body were being torn apart— he wanted to kiss Riley and to believe him—but he knew the hurt that came with believing an addict and it stopped him from knowing what to do.

"And by the way, you of all people should know that addicts are good at hiding stuff. You've assumed I haven't been drinking because you haven't seen me take a drink from one of the wait staff. When So You Think performed in Dubai, a dry city, I had vodka in my water bottle."

Vince stepped backwards. "What are you saying?"

"I'm saying you shouldn't judge people based on what you think you can see, or any preconceived ideas that you've formed because you knew someone else once. I am not your dad." Riley turned around and walked away, leaving Vince staring at the space he'd left. He pressed his fingers against his temples, unable to work out if Riley was drunk or not. Trust Riley to put him further off balance. He wasn't sure how long he stood there alone.

"Are you alright?" Jamie leaned against him and he tensed so he didn't shake her off. She didn't need that. "You look like you are going to murder someone."

"What?"

Jamie jerked away and he forced himself to relax his face

muscles. His jaw ached a little as if he'd been clenching it all evening.

"Sorry. I won't hurt you."

"I know. Now tell me what the problem is."

"If I knew what the problem was, it wouldn't be a problem."

She reached up and brushed his hair off his forehead. "Vince. I've never seen you like this."

"Like what?"

Her gaze darted sideways, then back to him. "You know, not cool, calm and collected. You're all wound tight and angry."

"Did I ever tell you how brave you are?"

She blinked quickly. "I'm not brave. Not at all."

"Yes you are. You must know the rumours about you, and yet you attend every function with your head held high, immaculately dressed with impeccable manners."

"Thank you. I think that's what hurts the most about… Craig. I've spent all evening thinking about him and how much I'm a desperate fool. Father pushed us together and I ignored every red flag about Craig because even after everything, I still want to impress Father. Now I'm the one who will pay the price. Again."

"I'll look after you, as a friend. I promise." Vince knew exactly what she meant. He'd spent his whole childhood trying to get his father to love him, but his bloody father had loved being off his head more than anything else.

"But who will look after you?"

Vince closed his eyes for a second. As much as he wanted to ignore the image of Riley naked on his couch, he couldn't. "What are you talking about? I don't need anyone."

"Who is he?"

It took Vince a moment to process what Jamie meant. "You know?" He'd kept it quiet because he hadn't worked out what impact being openly gay would have on Kapow's financial position. He liked certainty, and being open wouldn't give him that.

"Vince. I'd always wondered, and then you pretty much confirmed it before." Her wobbly intake of breath was loud. 'Why do you think we've always been friends?"

"I… What?"

"I'm—" Jamie leaned in close and whispered. "—queer too. Probably bisexual or pansexual. I just haven't had the space to work that out yet."

"Your father would hate it."

"No shit, Sherlock." She kissed him on the cheeks as a camera flash went off. "No. Stop. I can't talk about it here and besides, I want to know who has broken your heart."

"No one. Don't be absurd." He didn't have a heart that could get broken.

She giggled. "I think you protest too much."

"I don't love… I just—" Feel too much around him and had fucked everything up. He prided himself on being able to read people and he'd messed up by assuming Riley was exactly like his father because he didn't want to go through that same heartbreak over and over again. Shit. Riley had known—had taunted him with it to see how he'd respond— and he'd screwed that up too.

"Sure you don't. That's why your gaze is tracking

someone around the room, and you look like you'll punch anyone who talks to him."

He didn't do that. He was just keeping his eye on his client because… He moved his head to stare at her, and it took a lot of effort. Fuck. He wanted Riley more than he should. From the first time he'd heard his sultry voice on the CD stuck in his car, he'd wanted him. His offer in the parking garage was too good to be ignored even though somewhere deep in his brain he knew this would happen, knew that he'd fall for Riley.

"O. M. G. I never thought I'd see the day. Vince Cattaneo brought down by love."

"Shoosh."

"Did you just shoosh me? It's worse than you thought." The glee on her face almost made the humiliation worthwhile.

"Fine. But now what? I messed up?"

Jamie grinned and jabbed him in the ribs with her elbow. "Come on. Not as much of a mistake as I've made." She blew out an unsteady breath.

"Why don't you leave?"

"My father or Craig?"

"The former. Craig is not worth your time."

She looked nervously around the room. "If I don't do as I'm told, he punishes Mum. I can't abandon her." Jamie confirmed all the rumours and he wanted to bundle her up in a hug, or something uncharacteristically emotional.

"Shit, Jamie. I'm so sorry. What do you need?"

"Not here. Let's sort out your broken heart first."

"It's not broken. God, you are so fucking dramatic."

She grinned. "Sure. I'm so dramatic. My life is a disaster but at least I didn't love Craig."

"Yeah." He mumbled. He didn't love Riley, it was just…

"What?" Jamie's eyes widened.

"Nothing." Shit. He needed to sit down because the truth hit him like a sack of potatoes dropped from a second storey balcony. He did love Riley. The weight of his judgement against Riley grew heavier. He had to fix this and prove that he'd been wrong about all addicts being the same.

17

"Good news." When Uma called a week after the industry dinner party in Sydney, she didn't bother to say hi. The excitement in her voice made him grin. "Someone pulled out of the big Sydney New Year's show in the Domain, and you've been offered their spot."

"Yes." This was the beginning of a new path for him. He didn't need Vince, or anyone to hold him back. Performing his new music in front of a crowd was exactly what he wanted. He would go forward with zero regrets—he'd said his piece to Vince at the dinner party and Vince hadn't reacted. If he truly meant his apology, surely he would've called or texted or emailed or one of the myriad of other communication tools that existed. Radio silence on that front told Riley everything he needed to know. The real problem was that it hurt like the blazers and it shouldn't. Riley had rejected Vince, not the other way around. He shouldn't be feeling this regret or whatever it was preventing him from wanting to eat. Damn it. He'd spent a week circling over everything they'd said and done since meeting each other and there wasn't much he would change. If he'd talked to Vince earlier about his addiction it wouldn't have mattered, because Vince was the one who'd held back crucial information and then been unwilling to discuss the impact it had had on his life. Riley didn't blame him. Living with an addict was impossible; trying to love one was even harder. He'd had the benefit of therapy for himself, and his own family had been on that journey with him. He was lucky to have them support him even when they didn't really under-stand him. If only Vince had been willing to let down his walls a little and talk about it. What they had was good, a unique connection of mind and body, but he knew he couldn't push Vince. He couldn't force him to talk about it if he wasn't ready. If only waiting for him didn't suck so much.

"I already said yes, because they wanted an urgent answer or they'd offer the spot to someone else. I hope you didn't mind, but I couldn't get hold of you earlier."

"That's fine. It's your job to sort out bookings like that. By the way, I finish up at the council tomorrow, so my schedule will be easier for you to plan." Without a backup income, everything rode on his music which was both a thrill and a disaster. His body flushed hot, then cold. If only he had a partner who he could share all his concerns with. Why the fuck did everything lead back to Vince? So much for no regrets. If Vince had done something terrible, he could've moved to a different marketing company and put it all behind him. Empathy for Vince's childhood was a clamp around his chest, a belt done up too tight, and all he wanted to do was find a solution so they could build on their initial connection and make it real and forever. Shit.

"I know, Bryce told me."

"So you guys are good now?"

"Yeah."

"Awesome. I haven't seen him so happy in ages. I'm glad you guys are cool." Riley hadn't decided if he would stay in Bourke or move to the city yet. He didn't need to be in expensive city housing when there was an airport at Bourke and he was still at the very beginning of this new career path. That was mostly bullshit though—he didn't want to be in the same city as Vince where he could be rejected over and over again—except that was also untrue. Vince was too bloody stubborn to reject him more than once. They were already over. His throwaway lust driven line about having sex to get it out of their system had come to fruition and Riley was the only one who'd fallen too hard and wanted more.

He clenched his fist. Being in the city was the most sensible solution for his career. Last time, with So You Think, their music had taken off almost instantly because they'd had the backing and marketing of a huge record label. The boy band had been designed to go global and So You Think began touring almost the day after signing their contracts. This time around there was a slower build up toward success. He'd been getting good sales on the new song without breaking records, and he had worked out a timetable for new releases with Uma who was doing an amazing job on the marketing.

"Thanks. We are taking it slow for now, what with the

distance and stuff. He's been searching for jobs nearer to me, but it's not that simple."

"Good luck. I remember you mentioned that." Perhaps he could move to the city once Bryce got a job there and they could stay flatmates. He could ease back into city life with a mate beside him.

"Thanks."

"I hope you guys can work it out." Unlike himself and Vince. Bloody Vince was too stubborn, too rigid in his thinking to apologise, and the whole thing had petered out before it had had a chance. A bright flame with no fuel to keep it burning that was more like lightning than a sustainable heat source.

"So do I. Anyway, I'll email you all the things you need for this concert and once I get it confirmed, we can sort out the contracts with Ella, and get it updated on your website and socials." Uma had been promoted recently to handle his entire client package with Kapow, and she'd really thrived with the extra responsibility. Her hard work allowed him space to focus on the music, although since he'd come back to Bourke after the Christmas party last week, everything had been too melancholy. He had to find a way to get over Vince before it impacted on the vibe of his new album.

"Super. Chat later." He waited until she hung up, and then sat down heavily on his couch. Emotions had always been the key driving force behind his music; hence why he'd become entrapped by alcohol when he was in So You Think. It was so much easier to maintain the lively energy the band needed with a skin full of drink to take away his anxiety. When drunk, he worried less about what other people thought of him, and if it went a bit overboard at times, it was worth it. Riley closed his eyes. Yeah, until it hadn't been worth it. A loud knock on the door made him leap to his feet.

"Coming." Gees, whoever it was didn't have to bash the door down. He opened the door and there was Vince. In Bourke. "Um, hi."

"Hello. Can I come in?"

"Sure." Riley stepped aside to let Vince into his house.

"Fuck me. It's not much cooler in here than outside."

Riley shook his head. "That's not true at all. The fans are doing their best to keep the heat from being ridiculous."

"I don't know how you can live out here. It's so much hotter than in Sydney."

"Did you come all this way to criticise my town?"

Vince chuckled and his shoulders lost a little bit of tension. "Of course not. I came here to apologise. You were right, Riley."

"I know."

Vince blinked slowly. "I'm sorry that I projected my past onto you."

"It's okay." Riley wanted to get this done with so they could move onto more important things, like working out what came next. Like make up sex. He swallowed. They needed to talk about how this might work, all those pesky details like…

"It's really not okay. I'd like to try and have a long term relationship with you and it's not okay for you to dismiss my apology."

"I'm not dismissing anything. I meant that it's okay, or

rather, it's natural to assume that I might hurt you just as your Father obviously hurt you—" Riley watched as Vince stiffened, as if he were putting on armour. "—Stop doing that. Just because I have some information about you and your father and then I applied logic to that information to reach the conclusion that he'd hurt you…" He guessed at what Vince's reaction might mean. "That doesn't mean that everyone knows that."

Vince glanced sideways, then stared at him with those piercing brown eyes. "I suppose this is the point where I tell you the whole fucking sob story and we…"

"Have sex?" Riley was hopeful.

Vince crumpled over, his shoulders shaking, and Riley rushed over to help him. "That's why I adore you." Vince lifted his face with a giant grin plastered across it.

"You were laughing?" Fucking hell, Riley had assumed Vince was crying like the sob story he was reluctant to tell and he'd leaped to comfort him. His heart pounded in his chest as if he'd run up three flights of stairs while holding his breath.

"Yes. I spent the whole flight here stressed about this apology and as soon as I saw you standing in your house, every word disappeared because I just wanted to kiss you. It took all my control to stick to my plan. Why do you put me off balance so easily?"

Riley ignored the questions because he felt exactly the same way about Vince. "Your plan was to bitch about the heat?"

Vince's eyes sparkled. "Better that than grab you and kiss you when I didn't know if that's what you wanted."

"It's what I want."

Vince's eyes flared wide and Riley heard the sharp intake of his breath. A rush of heat spread across his body and he waited for Vince's kiss. It didn't happen, instead Vince blinked once and his demeanour switched from hungry to controlled. It was impressive how he could command a room with a look and Riley almost sank to his knees in front of him.

"But first, I need to talk." Vince wiped his brow with a silk handkerchief and eased out a long breath.

"It's okay. I can wait." He didn't want to wait. He would because he'd suddenly realised that Vince was nervous. He hid it so well under his uniform of corporate deal maker.

"I have to say this."

"Please continue." Riley pushed away the sudden need for a drink. Damn, that screaming sensation hadn't bugged him for years; the need for a crutch to ease through an awkward moment. Intellectually he knew the fight would never go away, and of course the desire would thrive when he was vulnerable. He stood up straight and stared at Vince and simply focused all his energy on the gorgeous wreck of a man standing in his lounge in a damned three piece suit on a fucking hot summer day. Being present for Vince mattered more than anything. The need for a drink flickered and faded. Good.

"Did you just bow?"

Riley cleared his throat. "Sorry. I didn't expect any of this and—"

Vince moved like a fucking panther and kissed him before he could end the sentence. Yes. This was what he'd been longing for. The kiss was rough and ready and desperate with tongues and teeth clashing. Vince's hands roamed all over his arms, shoulders, and back and Riley did the same. He needed to be skin to skin with Vince, and he grabbed his shirt and pulled it out of the way. His hands touched Vince's skin with a scorching heat and one of them —both of them—groaned.

"Oh my god. Why did I wait so long?"

Riley couldn't answer him, his breath had been stolen by Vince.

"I wanted you so much and it scared the pants off me." Vince's voice rasped too.

"I'll take your pants off without scaring you."

"Riley! I mean, yes, but I really want to apologise to you. I bloody ghosted you because I was too timid to care about you. And I'm never scared of anything." Vince growled at him and Riley kissed him on the forehead.

"You can't spend your whole life separate from emotional connection."

"Damn you. I was willing to try until I met you." Vince pulled Riley's hips closer to him and ground against him. "Why did it have to be you? Why couldn't it be someone who doesn't push all my buttons?"

Riley laughed, a deep chested uncontrolled laugh.

"What?"

"Vince. You were never going to fall for someone safe. You want me because I'm not safe. My past forces you to confront yours. We will probably always argue because we are two driven people who aren't content to live ordinary lives. My family often say they don't know where I came from because they are happy with their lot and I had to be famous. I had to be the life of the party, the centre of attention, the teen idol."

Vince let out a sigh strong enough to ruffle the papers on Riley's desk. "I don't want to fight with you anymore."

"It's inevitable given our personalities, so if this is going to work, we are going to have to accept that and figure out a way to resolve our clashes. Like with sex."

"Riley! Damn, I fucking love you."

"You do?" Riley had spent too long hoping to hear those words and they were everything he'd hoped for. So much so that a response stuck in his throat. "I mean, awesome, thanks. Same."

"Same?"

"Fucking shitballs. I mean—" There was only one way passed his awkward blurt. Riley kissed Vince and poured all his love and lust and his whole fucking heart into the kiss. He might have the words, the lyrics to their tune, but it was more than that. He could make both their bodies sing with desire.

"Same." Vince panted as he lifted his head and Riley couldn't stop the smile.

"Hey, I'm a song writer, not a poet."

"Isn't that the same thing?"

Riley buried his head against Vince's neck and breathed in his salty, spicey scent with that ever present hit of gin. Yes, together they'd be forced to confront their past. This was the home he wanted. With Vince. His love. The bassline picked itself out and he started to tap it against Vince's shoulders.

"It's hot in here. Take off your clothes." Riley traced his

fingers down the front of Vince's chest and undid his jacket.

"No."

"Excuse me? Weren't you just bitching about the heat and look at what you are wearing!"

"I came here to talk. Not to be used for cheap sex."

Riley grinned. "There's nothing cheap about me." He pushed Vince's jacket off his shoulders, then slid his hands down to his waist. He undid Vince's belt and all the buttons on his suit pants, then pushed them down to reveal Vince's gorgeous hard cock. He deliberately licked his lips and when Vince growled, a delicious shiver rushed down his spine.

"I know. You've dragged me on a journey that is priceless, pushing me to accept you even after all my doubts about addicts and everything."

Riley stroked his hand over Vince's hard cock. "Keep talking."

"Can't." The agony in Vince's voice was everything. He gripped Vince's cock tight, loving the silk of his skin under his palm. Since he'd been working on this album, his fingertips had hardened with callouses from the guitar strings and the contrast felt great. From the way Vince thrust into his hand, it was also amazing for Vince.

He breathed in deep, ready to talk. "You are a piece of work, Vince. I told you I wanted more than a once-off in a carpark, and you freaked out. Didn't talk to me for weeks." He pumped his hand on Vince's cock, in the rhythm of the new song rattling around his head. "And now you arrive on my doorstep with a declaration of love and expect me to agree without being confused."

"Gah."

"Right? It's not fair, but…" He paused, deliberately, because he loved teasing Vince like this. Loved seeing him off-balance. "It's all good. I love you Vince. The way you command a room when you are being the boss. The glare you give someone when you are trying not to say something sarcastic and mean. The way your knees are buckling now for me."

"You love me." It wasn't a question.

"Obviously." Riley answered anyway, then he dropped to his knees and angled Vince's cock into his mouth. The bare skin was a declaration. He swallowed the engorged cock, slipping it between his lips until Vince filled his mouth, and when Vince gripped his hair, he let him take charge and control the movement of his head. The tight prickles as Vince's fingers tangled in his hair added to the surge of sensation in his blood and on his skin. His own cock pressed hard against his pants and when Vince moved his foot to lift his toes against his balls, he groaned.

"Riley." Vince cradled his cheeks and lifted his face. "Take me to your bed." He pulled him to his feet, and they staggered down the hallway to Riley's bedroom.

"I missed you. Us. This."

"Damn." Vince's mouth seduced him as they kissed once more, the rich chaotic hint of juniper berries filling Riley's mouth with the taste of forever. He wanted this forever, knowing Vince would balance care with roughness just as he needed it. He pressed his body against the lean hardness of Vince and groaned into their kiss. An echo of his own moan gathered in the base of his chest, his heart quickening more than he might have imagined, and all the time, Vince's hands roamed, tangling with Riley's as he also tried to touch Vince everywhere.

"It's too bloody hot for these clothes." They broke the kiss for the necessary task of getting naked, working together with shaking hands, before they tumbled onto the bed. Vince wrapped his arms around Riley and pulled him close.

"It's almost too hot for sex."

"No."

"No. Not at all. I'd put up with more for you." Vince's lips grazed Riley's mouth, then slid down across his jaw and throat. Riley shivered and Vince chased the sensation with his hands until Riley groaned helplessly. It was all he could do but lie there and thread his hands through Vince's hair, holding onto him tight. Vince kept pressing hot kisses to random pieces of his skin, the small hollow of his collar bone, the spot left of his nipple, and when he dragged his lips across Riley's ribcage, Riley's hands slipped out of Vince's hair and grabbed his shoulders. Those broad muscular shoulders that carried all the weight of his past, his business, his drive, and his fortune.

"Mine." Riley had never been possessive, but damn, Vince made him want to keep him close forever. "I love you and you are all mine."

"Just took a few decent kisses."

Riley tried to agree, but somehow Vince sucked all the words out of his mouth by shifting between his legs. In the smoothest move, Riley had ever seen, everything in the world reduced to Vince's mouth surrounding his cock. He wanted to buck his hips and fuck Vince's mouth hard. The need was met when Vince pumped his mouth on his hard length until the pressure grew too much and Riley found the self-preservation from somewhere deep inside to shove his thumb in the corner of Vince's mouth.

"Stop."

Vince automatically sat up and held his hands up high.

"Oh." A fierce prickly warmth made all the hairs on his skin stand up. "Oh. Thank you."

"You said stop."

"I did. I didn't expect you to be so dramatic. I just didn't want to come in your mouth."

Vince grinned, the cocky world-owning smile that Riley fucking loved. "Consent matters."

"Then I consent to it all."

"All? Are you sure? I have quite the imagination."

Riley closed his eyes and groaned. Glad he was lying on a bed and not standing because his legs were weak with that declaration. "Yes. I want all of you. Claim me."

Vince's smile stretched and he stared hungrily at Riley all laid out on the bed. He lowered his hands, and the very first touch was to trace Riley's tattoo. When he'd had it done, he'd never imagined it would be used to tease him so mercilessly, because the way Vince traced his fingers along the musical notes drawn around the base of Riley's cock only emphasised that Vince wasn't touching his cock.

"More. Please."

Vince rested his palms on Riley's thighs, before he deliberately drifted one hand around the tattoo again, then cupped Riley's balls. He moaned. Vince let his hand slid down, and slowly slid one finger into his arse. The groan came from deep inside and he whispered. Hoarse.

"Lube in drawer."

Vince shifted, and Riley half sat up to grab at him and keep him close. He needn't have bothered, as Vince quickly covered his cock with a condom and squirted lube onto his hands and gently prepared him for sex. The slow steady preparation wasn't enough. Riley squirmed against Vince's hand, needing more, and not having the breath to ask for it.

"Riley." His name tore through the air as Vince slowly pushed his cock inside, filling Riley until he begged and cried out. The relief of having him there built against sheer impatience. He wanted Vince hard and rough and full and he used his arms and legs to pull him closer. Yes, that sensation of being filled by him was everything. The rightness of it and the bliss on Vince's face felt like the beginning of a life together.

"Good?" That Vince even had the ability to ask seemed incredible as Riley lost all semblance of logical thought.

"Great. I want more."

Vince kissed him hard, gently rocking until Riley arched his back and begged with his body. Vince changed his rhythm like a nineties rock song. Fast, slow, fast. Hard, gentle, hard. Until Riley was completely undone by it, and he couldn't hold on anymore. He ripped his mouth from Vince's kiss and buried his face against Vince's neck as he came hard against Vince's bare stomach. Vince followed him with a roar, collapsing onto Riley's body, and the bright shards of his own finish sang inside his head like the encore performance at a rock concert. Sex was better with love, a true pleasure that mattered more than the chemical rush of two bodies meeting.

"Let me clean you up." Vince's voice was harsh, as if his roar of pleasure had stripped his vocal chords.

"Shower." Riley couldn't form more than one word. He spilled more than just come onto Vince and he didn't really have the energy to do more than lie in the heat.

"Come on, before this—" Vince waved his hand as he eased out of Riley's sated body, "—dries on."

Riley smiled as Vince cared for him, and let Vince lead him to the bathroom for a shower. Vince loved him. He deserved to be loved by someone who knew his past and could cope with it. Vince had proven himself worthy. He turned on the shower with a cynical grin. It was probably just the spectacular sex talking.

"I was wrong to assume all addicts are the same."

"Yes."

"I realised that I couldn't live without you. I need you and your snarky sense of humour. I love you, and I'll stand by you even if you fall off the wagon."

Riley's skin prickled all over again and he had to fight the urge to blurt something ridiculous. After a couple of breaths, he was ready. "Thank you. Your acknowledgement of that is perfect. I truly do love you. I love the way you are willing to be wrong even when you are mostly right all the bloody time."

Vince shrugged carelessly. "Arrogance is part of this package."

"And it's a fucking great one." Riley grinned and turned on the shower. "Time for round two." This time, he'd be inside Vince and he'd shower him—literally—with all the love pumping in his veins.

18

Vince hadn't been to a family dinner since his beloved grandfather died and he'd gone a little overboard buying presents for Riley's family. A puzzle for his mum, bottle of very expensive wine for his dad, and a voucher for a spa treatment for his older sister. And yes, he might have also bought something for Riley's sister's husband and a couple of presents for Riley's nieces. He grabbed the box out of the boot of Riley's 4WD and carried it to the front door of the suburban Federation cottage in western Sydney. The entire street was so typically Australian in a way that was foreign to his inner city life. Comfortable and homely. His throat was thick as he followed Riley to the front door, then inside. An older man who was so obviously related to Riley stretched out his hands.

"Here, let me take those."

"Thanks Dad."

Vince handed over the box. "Careful, it's a bit heavy."

"I'll be fine. I'm not as decrepit as I look." Riley's Dad took the box easily and winked at Vince.

"Hello Riley. Who is your friend?"

Vince put out his hand for a shake. "I'm Riley. I mean, I'm Vince, Riley's friend."

Riley grinned. "Vince is my life partner, not just a friend."

"Oh. No wonder he was so nervous he introduced himself as you." The woman, presumably Riley's mum, grinned.

"I'm never going to live that down, am I?"

"It's not the most embarrassing thing my son has ever done, so I wouldn't stress about it."

"Mum." Riley pulled his mum into a hug. "You promised me you wouldn't tell any embarrassing stories."

"Did I?" With two simple words, Vince could see exactly where Riley got his sense of humour from. His mum reacted in that same way that always seemed to knock Vince off balance. "Vince, welcome to the family. Please call me Katy."

"Hi Katy. Thanks for inviting me to lunch."

"It's our pleasure. Riley told us you don't have family around you for Christmas."

"Mum. I told you that his family was off-topic."

Vince shrugged one shoulder. "It's okay. I was brought up by my grandparents, but they died years ago, so it's just been me for a while now."

"You are always welcome here. Please come all the way inside and grab something to eat or drink."

Hours later, all the presents had been handed out and most of the food eaten. Vince leaned back on the couch with his arm slung around Riley's shoulders.

"Who is ready for our annual Christmas tradition?" Riley's Dad, George, stood beside the television.

Riley leaned closer and whispered to Vince. "Be careful, we don't have any traditions."

"I heard that. And I'm starting a new tradition as of today."

"Oh God." Riley's sister Leila laughed. "Is this going to be like the year you made everyone say something nice about everyone in the room? That was torture."

"It shouldn't be torture to say nice things about someone."

"It is when Riley just said "I like their hair" to everyone."

Riley roared with laughter. "Hey, I was six. What else was I going to say?"

Vince jumped to his feet. "I want to say something. Meeting Riley has given me so much joy, and today has been truly amazing. For a long time now, I've been without a family to share Christmas Day with and I'm so honoured that you've all welcomed me into your home and treated me as part of the family." He paused, not wanting to say how not every family would've been so openly happy to have a gay man in their house. He wasn't going to put a negative note on a wonderful day. "So that's it really. Thank you. I appreciate it."

"It's our pleasure. I think I speak for the whole family when I say I'll always welcome someone who makes our

Riley happy. It's been a long and interesting road being involved in Riley's life—"

"Dad!" Riley's protest was met with laughter.

"Well, it has. You were an intense teenager who wasn't content to learn one instrument, you begged us for lessons for piano, guitar, and saxophone, and then you taught yourself the drums and that thing on the computer."

"A mixer."

"And well, then there was a pop star phase which wasn't something we were really equipped to be part of, but it was also amazing when it went well."

"Um, we don't need to talk about the next part. I'm sorry I didn't involve you in my rehabilitation, but it's a pretty personal journey and—"

"But you did involve us. We went to many therapy sessions with you."

"I know. I appreciate it. Look, I know I didn't make the same choices as you."

"Son, I've never been worried about that. Only worried about you. You were always destined to shine brightly and it's no surprise to us that you've picked a partner like Vince who is so comfortable in his own skin and obviously successful."

"Thank you. I think he's pretty great too." Riley winked and Vince chuckled.

"To us, and to many wonderful Micah Christmas days together."

AUTHOR NOTES

This book was written during the COVID19 pandemic that made 2020 so difficult for some many people around the world. I've deliberately ignored the pandemic in this book because the first two books in this series were written in 2017, so it suited me to continue in a world ignorant of the pandemic. Readers can either pretend the book is set before the pandemic or pretend it doesn't exist in this fictional world. Whatever works for you. As we live through a moment in history, I find it difficult to put the pandemic into a book as it's hard to see how the world might be changed by the pandemic. The length of the publishing cycle doesn't lend itself well to dealing with current events.

My thoughts are with anyone who has lost someone to COVID19.

ALL BOOKS BY RENÉE DAHLIA

Thanks for reading CRAVING HIS SPOTLIGHT. I hope you enjoyed it.

If you'd like to know more about me, my books, or to connect with me online, you can visit my webpage www.reneedahlia.com and if you sign up to my newsletter, you can grab a free book Ode to the Banh Mi.

Twitter https://twitter.com/dekabat

Facebook https://www.facebook.com/reneedahliawriter/

Instagram   https://www.instagram.com/reneedahlia_author/

Reviews can help readers find books, and I am grateful for all honest reviews. Thank you for taking the time to let others know what you've read, and what you thought.

You've just read a book in my Kapow series. The other books in this series are:

1. Out of Her League (fm with bisexual characters)
2. Rekindled (ff) Short Story (also included as a bonus in Out of Her League)
3. His Buxom Beauty (fm)
4. Craving His Spotlight (mm)
5. Her Pregnant Rival (ff) (Feb 2021)

If you liked this book, here are my other books:

Contemporary Series: Farrellton Foster Family

1. Betrayed (fm)
2. Liability (ff)
3. Forbidden (fm with bisexual characters)

Contemporary Series: Merindah Park

1. Merindah Park (fm)
2. Making Her Mark (fm with bisexual heroine)
3. Two Hearts Healing (fm)
4. Racetrack Royalty (fm)

Contemporary Series: Rainbow Cove

1. His Christmas Pearl (fm)
2. His Christmas Pride (mm)

Contemporary Series: Homage

1. Ode to the Banh Mi (fm with bisexual heroine)

2. Uplift (ff with bisexual heroines): Only One Bed anthology (KU)

Historical Series: Great War Ladies

1. Her Lady's Honor (ff)

Historical Series: Bluestockings

0.5 The Shipwrecked Earl's Bride (fm with bisexual hero): 12 Rogues of Christmas anthology (KU)

1. To Charm a Bluestocking (fm with bisexual hero)
2. In Pursuit of a Bluestocking (fm)
3. The Heart of a Bluestocking (fm)